Fighting Blood

FIGHTING BLOOD

·

WILLIAM HEYLIGER

·

The Goldsmith

Publishing Company

CHICAGO

Contents

Fighting Blood

A Shadow Dawns

His name was Ball—Tarly Nicholas Theodore Ball. Quite a name. Quite a boy.

The good things of life had always fallen into his lap. His people had money. Nature had given him vim, endurance, supple muscles and a strong frame. His family had given him the comforts that money could buy. He had never had to fight for anything.

And yet, strangely, he was a fighter.

He had a crisp swirl of red hair and a wild flame of battle in his eyes. He carried his head high and he wore clothes well. He walked lightly on his toes like an athlete, and he had a proud swagger-sway to his hips. He had been born a Somebody and he didn't intend that the world should forget it.

While he was still in grammar school the crowd called him TNT. Already he was recognized as an explosive. The *Mountain Argus* ran a solo story about him with a picture. That was after he had scored four touchdowns in a grammar school game. After that stories concerning TNT Ball began to pop into the newspaper more or less regularly. He didn't have to go out of his way to convince the world he was a Somebody. The world had already discovered that interesting fact.

As a result, when he went on to Mountain High, he had acquired a reputation. He had always thought well of one Tarley Ball. Now his self-esteem went up several notches and he began to think extraordinarily well of himself. The flame of battle in his eyes became a trifle wilder. He had begun to look upon himself as one of those Somebodys who "had something" and who could "get away with it."

That kind of thinking in a boy is apt to prove dangerous.

Once at Mountain High, Fate served notice that she had marked him out for those attentions she lavishes upon her warm favorites. There was no first year ineligibility rule at Mountain and he did the unheard of thing of making the school football team his freshman year. Though playing with and against boys much older than himself, he stood out. Once again the *Argus* ran a solo story with a new picture. The old TNT faded into the dust of forgotten designations. He found himself wrapped in the glory of a newer, a more colorful name.

Cannonball! Cannonball Ball!

Luck played a part in all that, as luck so often plays a part in the affairs of the extremely fortunate. Tarly used to throw back his red head and chant something about how strange it was luck usually followed a player full of the old fight. He prided himself upon the fact that when it came to a football fight he could do his stuff regardless of the odds.

Ordinarily he would have been a good, likely freshman who would have been counted on by a coach to develop in a year or two. Where luck played into his hands was in that Mountain High did not really have a coach. They had a man named Malcolm Cudleigh who bore the title of coach, but the title was rather empty. It was always a question just how deep his knowledge of and his interest in football were. He taught physics and chemistry at the high school; the Board of Education paid him one hundred dollars extra a year to handle the team. It was not much of a salary and Mr. Cudleigh did not bother to give the team much of his time. His principal responsibility seemed to be to travel with the squad to and from its out-of-town games and see that none of the boys got into mischief.

His spare hours were more profitably spent in study and in writing articles for some scientific magazines. He came to the field two or three times a week, stayed around a while and then disappeared and went back to his writing desk. The team, left almost leaderless and inspirationless, wallowed along in a sort of torpid apathy.

It had caught the losing habit. That was bad enough. But there was something worse—the team didn't care.

That was the bleak situation when Tarly Nicholas Theodore Ball burst upon the scene.

It wasn't in the boy to take a licking and show any liking for the humiliation. In a world where other players came to the practice at a time that best suited their convenience—or didn't come at all—he was always on time. Mr. Cudleigh, on the days that he did appear, hovered about as though to crowd a lot of work into a few minutes, gave a few orders and departed unnoticed. Sometimes the orders were carried out. A lot depended upon how the players happened to feel that day. Sometimes the players shrugged, looked at each other, laughed and forgot Mr. Cudleigh's instructions. With nobody there to check them, such indifference was to be expected.

But day by day a red-headed dynamo worked as though his personal fate, his entire future, depended upon that afternoon's practice. The other players softened; he toughened and grew hard. When he tackled he tackled violently; when he carried the ball he went into the boy who tried to bring him down with a wild sweep of fighting joy. Scrub players, not finding this to their liking, became demoralized and faded from sight. Presently it was often found impossible to muster eleven players for the scrub team.

One boy of the scrubs, Joe Macy, was as tenacious as the imperial Tarly. He, too, came back day after day, and on time. He played left half; and as Tarly made hash of the line, his was often the task of bringing the red dynamo down. And very, very often he brought him down with a crash.

Tarly had a habit, after going down, of being the first to his feet and holding out a hand to his opponent as though the other boy needed aid. Joe never accepted the hand.

"Hurt you?" Tarly would ask.

And Joe would answer: "You all right?"

This little, private two-man feud in time got under the skin of Tarly Ball.

"You can take it, Joe," Tarly said one day as though conferring a benediction.

"You've taken a bit of it yourself," Joe Macy drawled.

Tarly Ball's intense dislike of Joe Macy could be dated from that hour.

The team, the season Tarly joined it, had a poor year. Not quite as poor, perhaps, from the point of scores as other years had been, but still decidedly poor. Week by week the team crept through its schedule; week by week an unbroken succession of defeats went down into the record. Southside, one of their important rivals, swept over Mountain for a 21-0 victory. Valley High, the ancient rival of all rivals, ploughed its way to a 40-0 triumph. The score might have been much greater but for Tarly Ball.

His was the only head unbeaten and unbowed. Plunging through the heavier Valley line, straight-arming interference, heaving, dodging, squirming for that last desperate foot of distance, he was a soul-stirring picture of a fighting man calculated to fill the eye and the imagination. On defense he roamed the line, plunging for the dynamited holes, spreading himself wide and low at the mouth of the openings to halt the irresistible Valley tide. But one man, even though that man be a Tarly Ball, could not do it all. The final whistle that marked a 40-0 defeat for Mountain High did not in the least dim his personal greatness.

As a matter of fact he came out of the game a hero. He was Horatius at the Bridge.

After that the team went through a formality. The players elected him captain. There was nothing else to do; there was nobody else to elect. He, who had been the first Mountain High freshman ever to make the team, now became the first man to captain that team in his sophomore year.

The election brought him another feature story in the *Argus*. He was accumulating quite a file of clippings and had bought a scrapbook.

"Fellows," he said, "It's about time Mountain High walked out in the center of the road."

The team shouted a stereotyped "Yeah!" There had been nobody else to elect; now there was nothing for them to do but to shout agreement to anything Tarly might say.

"I'm tired of being walked on. How about you? Do you want more of it?"

The dutiful team cried: "No."

"Neither do I. Come on, fellows. Bare your backs. Dig in your heels and put up the stop sign. We can do it."

Somebody shouted: "Hurrah! That's talking, Tarly."

A stir ran through the squad.

"It's only necessary to go out there and fight. F-I-G-H-T. An old Mountain fight. I'm going out there to fight from the first whistle to the last. Do you want me to fight alone?"

There was a babel of confused shouts and cries.

"Are you with me? Are you going to fight shoulder to shoulder with me?"

"Yeah!" came a yell from the aroused team. "We'll be with you all the way." Something magnetic, something inspiring and blood-stirring in Tarly Ball had caught them.

There was a two-year calendar on the wall. Tarly went to the calendar and flipped over pages. He came to a month. The month was September. He ran a circle with a red pencil around that entire page of the calendar.

"Let's remember that," he cried, "next September."

A day later the newly-elected captain went to call upon Malcolm Cudleigh.

"Mr. Cudleigh," he said, "I want to talk about next season."

"Ah—— Next season, did you say?" Mr. Cud-leigh seemed startled. "I have some writing to do——"

"I won't keep you but a few minutes," Tarly said. He was an insistent soul on having his own way. "I think that if we spread the line more next season, work out a few plays to perfection and depend upon speed——" He drew out paper and began to diagram plays.

Mr. Cudleigh glanced helplessly at the clock.

Three hours later Tarly departed. The teacher-coach went to his study, glanced ruefully at the work he had accomplished that night, covered the typewriter and went up to bed.

"Martha," he sighed to his wife, "I'm afraid I'm going to have trouble with that young man. He doesn't seem to be rational. He's a fanatic."

When the following September came the team remembered its promise. True, there were aspects that at first riled Captain Tarly Ball. On time himself, he chafed waiting for players to arrive. Practice that should have started at three-thirty o'clock usually got under way half-an-hour later. He made one or two attempts to enforce punctuality, but there he ran against a rock wall. In the end he wisely let the situation ride. While cold indifference to a starting time wasn't to his liking, there were other values. He was shrewd enough to appreciate them. After all, it was impossible to rout a settled system in a day. A football team wasn't a jail, and so long as the players worked once they got started——

That was the miracle. The team was putting its back into the job as it had never done before. Tarly, from last year's experience, could appreciate the change. He awoke to the knowledge that he had in him the sublime power to move men and to make them want to give their best. A flame ran through him.

Mr. Cudleigh found himself caught in a mad, foaming whirlpool of unaccustomed activity.

"Martha," he complained to his wife, "I was wrong about that young man, Tarly Ball. He is far worse than a fanatic. He is a lunatic."

Things were happening too fast for a man who came to the field briefly a few times a week and went through a show of earning one hundred dollars. All at once Mr. Cudleigh no longer gave orders. Tarly would say: "I've shifted So-and-So to left end," and the teacher-coach would nod. Sometimes he wasn't quite sure if he knew who So-and-So was. Tarly said: "I'm going to drill them on the forward passing game. We may waste some downs, but if we keep passing that will force them to open up and our weight won't then count so much against us." Again Mr. Cudleigh nodded. And there came a day when Tarly said:

"We're due to pick the starting team, Mr. Cudleigh. Suppose I come around to your house tonight?"

"Why, eh—— Tonight?" Mr. Cudleigh edged away. "Suppose you make out a suggestive list, Tarly, and let me see it. I have an important engagement tonight."

Tarly made out the list. Mr. Cudleigh looked it over at practice next afternoon.

"Quite all right," he said. "Quite. Exactly the selections I should have made."

After practice, that afternoon, Tarly read the starting line-up to the squad. Ben Parks had been selected to play left-half. Joe Macy, again a candidate for the backfield, looked at Tarly out of hard, expressionless eyes.

"You're not quite ripe yet, Joe," Tarly said with an outward sign of friendliness.

Joe continued to look at him.

"A little later, perhaps——"

"Don't kid me," Joe answered shortly. "I wasn't born yesterday."

"I'm glad to hear it," Tarly said sweetly.

"There's always a chance of making the team tomorrow."

The luck that had followed Tarly Ball to Mountain High still walked in friendship at his shoulder. The team won three of its early games and then struck gold. Three of Southside's first-string men were hurt in an automobile accident and Mountain High ran wild against a crippled opponent and won easily. Just before the Valley game Valley's star triple-threat man was barred because of academic deficiencies, and Mountain High, playing far beyond its own power, scraped through to a heart-breaking 14-13 victory.

The Merchants' Association gave the team a
dinner in the Town Hall. Nobody could remember back to when any other Mountain team had
been so signally honored. Tarly, who had been re-
elected captain, made a speech and promised glory.
When the dinner came to an end he left the banquet
hall with Mr. Cudleigh.

"What about next year?" he asked.

A season of astounding events had left Mr. Cudleigh jarred and shaken. He preferred his academic
calm.

"You've done mighty well, Tarly," he said. "I'm
going to leave next season to you."

Tarly could have wished for nothing better.

He found the mantle of authority sweet. He
walked a little lighter on his toes and his smile was
the careless smile of a slowly growing confidence.
Not that he had lacked confidence before. Only
now he was beginning to look upon himself as in-
fallible and indispensible.

At first, when his third season started, he made a
short, strong attempt at enforcing punctuality.
This failed, as the effort had failed once before. He

gave it up. Why interfere with a system that was winning? For the first week he went through the formality of consulting with Mr. Cudleigh; gradually he ceased to consult him at all. Why bother with something that was merely a waste of time? His became the final word—on the make-up of the team, the plays, the signals, the strategy of the games.

Ben Parks again went to left-half; once more Joe Macy stayed with a scrub that had learned to take its daily pounding.

And Mountain High, hitting a stronger stride, won its games that second season, by larger and larger scores.

"I'm making a fighting team of it," Tarly exulted. "I, alone. All by myself."

Subtly, cautiously, he fed this viewpoint to Christy Lee, editor of the school weekly, *The Mountain Goat.*

"I suppose you think I'm lucky, Christy?"

Christy hastened to deny the charge.

"This team was always good. It—— Well, you know, it just didn't have the old fight. It was up to somebody to go in there and give it the fighting spirit."

"And you're the man who did it," Christy vowed.

Tarly shrugged modestly. "*I'm* not saying that, Christy. They're your words, not mine."

Christy, picking the thought up hungrily, wrote of Tarly as "the greatest fighting captain the orange and black has ever known." Those words "fighting captain" had a sound. And presently the school was deliriously singing a new song for which Christy wrote the words, "The Fighting Captain of a Fighting Team."

Tarly, eyes flashing, threw back his head and laughed a contented laugh deep down in his throat. He often threw back his head and laughed these days.

In his freshman year he had joined a team admittedly poor. But three years of following a torch had given it a flame of its own, welding it cohesively and ripening it. The team had, in some way and in some fashion, done what sports writers call "arrived."

Football experts began to say, over their signatures, that here was a team that, in another year, might write itself down into the records as one of the best scholastic teams of its generation.

"See what they're saying around the State," Tarly asked Christy Lee. "I mean, about the team?"

"Great, isn't it?" the editor beamed.

"I thought—— Oh, well, what's the use. You know your business better than I can tell it to you."

"What were you thinking, Tarly?"

"Oh, it's nothing. It might not be worth a rap. Anyway, you'd probably think I had a nerve——"

"Why should I? Gosh, you don't know how hard it is to get out a school paper and make it newsy. I suppose I get so close to the job at times that I don't see possibilities. What were you thinking about, Tarly?"

"I—— You won't laugh?"

"Of course not."

"Well, I thought if you gathered these opinions, made a sort of symposium, something like 'What Others Say of Us'—— Do you see what I mean?"

"Gosh!" said Christy. "I should have thought of

that myself. I can make it a feature and run it, black-face, in a box. Thanks for calling it to my attention, Tarly."

Christy gathered these opinions diligently, and ran them on the first page of the *Goat*, and Tarly eagerly read them and clipped each issue. He had been fed so long on praise that now it had become heady meat and he hungered for more of it. His vanity, slowly fed through three seasons, had at last become a consuming desire.

"This lad Christy," he told himself, "has been worth-while, and may continue to be worth cultivating. He's done me a clever turn here and there. I think it is up to me to look around for a place where I can do some small favor for him."

His vanity, after the fashion of vanity, had gone on another step. He was taking on the manner and the thought of royalty. He visioned himself rosily as one climbed to so vast a height that now he had favors at his command to bestow or to withhold.

Mountain High won the Valley game that year. This time there was no question of a hollow victory, for the orange and black swarmed over the best team that Valley was able to send to the field. For the second year in succession the game was a bitter battle, and for the second year in succession the score was 14-13.

But this time the score was an honest score, a true valuation of the teams, and the game was a game truly won and earned.

Mountain High fought its way back to the gym through a howling, jubilant mob of well-wishers. Without waiting to take off soggy, steaming, sweaty equipment the players settled the question of next year's captain. McNichol, the quarterback, leaping to a bench, steadied himself and raised his hands.

"We have a job to do," he cried. "And what a job! Ready to do it?"

"Yeah!" came from the team.

"Any question of the man?"

"Tarly!" This time the roar of the team could be heard a city block away.

Tarly made them a speech.

In truth, it wasn't much of a speech for he was almost dead on his feet. Shortly after the start of

the final quarter he should have come out, but nobody was there to order him out. But what the
speech lacked in fire and spontaneity it made up in
dramatics. Standing there, hot and exhausted, his
face drained, his lips and eyes drawn, he was the
picture of a man who had fought himself out for
his team. "Yah, Tarly! Yah, fighting captain!"

However, Tarly had the elastic buoyancy and
recuperative powers of boyhood. A stinging
shower revived him and his mind bubbled. Who
else had ever been elected captain for three years
running? He felt that in his final year, as a senior,
he would reach the utmost pinnacle.

Out in the street he found Christy Lee anxiously
and impatiently waiting for news.

"Did they do anything, Tarly?"

"Captain again, Christy."

"The third time! I must get down to the *Argus*
with this. Next week we'll run it in the *Goat*, but
the *Argus* can break the story tomorrow. Got anything to say—an interview."

"You know I never say anything about myself,
Christy."

"I know; but in a story like this an interview helps."

"Well—— Suppose you cook something up yourself and quote me. You'll know how to do it."

Christy said: "The *Argus* will probably put this on the A. P. wire."

Tarly didn't know what the A. P. meant. However, it sounded good. Important. Or was it? He had to find out.

"What's the A. P.?"

"Associated Press. That means the story will be used on sports pages all over the United States."

Tarly tingled. So his fame was to spread. He was to become a celebrity.

"I think I'll bring down the cut I ran in the *Argus* last month," Christy went on. "If the screen is all right for them they may use it."

Tarly didn't know what "screen" might mean. A shrewd instinct told him it might have something to do with the mechanics of printing. He did not ask. The pride that was so strong a part of him would not permit him to show ignorance a second time.

Christy Lee misread his silence. "You wouldn't mind, would you, Tarly?"

Tarly Ball gave a theatrical, nicely restrained display of coy reluctance.

"I wish you'd let me use it. I'm paid space rates by the *Argus*. It runs up my bill."

Tarly made a magnanimous motion with his hand. "Oh, that's different. Of course, if you'll get anything out of it——" He left the sentence unfinished.

The desire to bestow something on Christy, some gift really princely, came to him again. He subjected the editor to a slow and critical appraisal.

Christy flushed. "Anything wrong with me?"

"Of course not. I was thinking—— Can you drop in and see me tomorrow, Christy?"

"Anything important? I mean, will it keep until I see you at school Monday?"

"Well——" Tarly gave the careless smile. "I thought it important enough to have you see me tomorrow."

"All right; what time?"

"After dinner. Say about two o'clock."

The Ball home was a comfortable, rambling house, set far back from a road lined with majestic maples. The porch was wide and pleasantly inviting. Christy Lee, climbing the steps of that porch at two o'clock the next day, found Tarly sitting there in the sun surrounded by a mountain of newspapers. The captain nodded toward a chair.

"Sit down, Christy. The papers gave the game a good notice, didn't they?"

Christy said eagerly: "I was looking through the exchanges at the *Argus*. The *Bee-Herald's* picked you for All-State."

"I expected that," said Tarly. Overnight he had ceased to be the man who never talked about himself. Sunday papers from five or six cities of the State, streaming his name across their columns, had routed his last shred of pretended modesty. Why sing low when everybody else was singing high?

Christy again was conscious of the slow, critical appraisal that had made him uncomfortable yesterday.

"Ever play football?" Tarly asked suddenly.

"Well, I tried to."

"What does that mean?"

"I guess you've forgotten. I went out for end in my freshman year—the year you first made the team—and they gave me the gate. I never went back. I thought I must have been an awful mess if I couldn't make the scrub that year."

"Things," Tarly said complacently, "weren't then the way they are now. No head, no plan, no purpose. There wasn't anybody there who had the—— Well, the spark, if you know what I mean."

The editor indicated that he knew exactly what the captain meant.

"You're built for an end. Those legs of yours ought to be able to cover ground and go down the field fast. Ever do any running?"

"Some."

"How's your wind?"

"Never bothers me."

"Good! An end never amounts to much after he loses his wind. All right then, Christy, here's why I brought you here today. I'm going to do something for you."

He let this piece of information soak in and

gloried in the silent raptness of Christy's anticipation.

"I'm going to put you on the team."

A longing, suppressed and chloroformed for three long years, leaped to Christy's eyes.

"You mean that, Tarly?"

"Say that again, Christy."

Christy felt the reproof.

"I—— Well, I thought—— Oh, you know. I thought you might be joking."

"I never joke about my team," Tarly said, "because I take my team seriously. You heard me say that I was going to put you on the team. That's exactly what I'm going to do. I'm going to make you an end."

Christy's eyes glowed.

"I made this team what it is," Tarly continued, "and now I'm going to make you. I'll train you through most of the summer. Personal training. By the time school opens in September you'll be able to take your place in the line."

The longing in the other boy's eyes wavered. "You're forgetting something, aren't you, Tarly?"

Tarly's eyes were chillingly aloof. "Am I?"

"I mean——"

"Exactly what do you think I'm forgetting?"

"I haven't played football in three years."

Tarly's hands made a royal gesture. "Who runs this team?"

"You do."

"Then suppose you let me do what worrying is needed. I said I'd make you an end."

Autumn chilled and became frozen winter. There were bob-sled parties on Three Turn Hill and ice-skating on the pond at the edge of the town. Mountain's basketball team had a successful season, won its sectional championship and went on to the State capital to be eliminated in the State tourney. Winter slowly thawed and became spring. The goal posts were taken down, and High School Field was given over to baseball, track and tennis.

Tarly Ball, watching the goal posts stored away, told himself it would not be long until September. He spent his days dreaming football. There were three books by football coaches on the shelves of the town library; he took them out, read them avidly, and made careful notes. Through the long, lengthening evenings he diagramed plays, moving blocks of wood upon the table in his room, building up an attack and then manipulating men and searching for the defense. When school closed in June he felt that he was free—from studies, free to give weeks and weeks to football. He caught Christy Lee on the wide circle of stone steps outside the main entrance.

"Going away this summer, Christy?"

The editor nodded. "I'm invited up to my uncle's farm for about two weeks."

"Don't make it any more than two weeks; I'm not a real miracle man. We need time. Better get away early and get back early. We have a football date."

The old longing was fire in Christy Lee's eyes. "I must get down to the *Argus* with the school closing story. I'll see you tomorrow—early."

But he saw the captain of the Mountain High eleven much sooner than that. Flushed and excited, he was back on the porch of Tarly Ball's home within an hour.

"Did the carrier bring your *Argus* yet, Tarly?" His hands were concealed behind his back.

Tarly sat up straight. Then, catching himself, he relaxed in the chair. It was poor policy to publicly show interest in the mere fact that his name might be in the paper again. He affected an air of bore-dom.

"Not yet."

"Then you haven't seen it?"

Tarly found it hard to restrain his interest in the face of Christy's excitement. He sighed.

"Good night! You don't mean to tell me they're riding my trail again?"

"W—well, not quite." The editor's hands came from behind his back holding a folded newspaper. A story on page one was enclosed in a firm circle of red pencil. "Read that."

Tarly read the short paragraph:

BASIL YORK NEW
PHYSICAL INSTRUCTOR

The Board of Education last night named Basil York as physical training instructor, his duties to begin with the opening of the new school year.

Heretofore the physical training instructor has supervised the compulsory physical training that is part of the curriculum of the town's schools. With the advent of Mr. York, the Board announced, the physical training instructor will also act as coach of high school athletics.

Mr. York has won an enviable reputation in the far west, his specialties being football and track.

Tarly Ball plopped the folded newspaper against one knee and put it down. His eyes had a wide-open stare of bland amusement. He smiled.

"Interesting," he commented.

"I bet a man like York will be able to teach this team something," Christy burst forth.

Tarly's eyes lost their bland, wide-open expression and closed to slits. "Do you think so?"

Christy was stumped. "Well—— Why not?"

"I'm asking you."

"You'd think with all his experience——"

"So that's it. Experience. Well, Christy, with all

his experience, just what will he be able to teach us?"

Christy's mouth hung open for a moment and a slow flush crept into his cheeks. Too late he saw where his rush of rash enthusiasm had led him.

"I didn't mean, Tarly——"

"Do you always have to explain what you mean?" Tarly asked softly. "Now, when I make a statement nobody can misunderstand it. When I said I'd make you an end I meant just that. And to get back to where we were, just what can this amazing Mr. Basil York teach us?"

"Why—— I don't know. I hadn't thought of it that way. What is there for him to teach us?"

Tarly's eyes lost their ominous slits and opened benignly. "Now you're asking yourself a sensible question. Everybody, I suppose, goes off half-cocked sometimes and jumps to conclusions. That's a mistake. Always think. Can this man teach us to win?"

Christy hastened to say: "Of course not. We don't need that kind of teaching. You're winning for us now."

"And how!" Tarly said with his head thrown back and that laugh in his throat. "No, Christy, he won't teach this team to win because I've already done that. I, Tarly Ball, all by myself. Do you know what he will do?"

The editor shook his head.

"He'll keep his hands off as Mr. Cudleigh did. That's not a criticism of Mr. Cudleigh and is not to be quoted. Mr. Cudleigh was all right; he knew that when he had a good man running things it might not pay to interfere. This York won't keep his hands off because of lack of interest, but because it will be wise. And do you know why that will be wise?"

Christy waited.

"It will be wise because he will find he has inherited a winning combination. When coaches find a winning combination—I mean new coaches having their first year—they let it alone. Why shouldn't they? Suppose they stick in a disturbing oar and the team immediately has a bad season? Who gets the potted palm? And if they stick in an oar and the team wins, what credit do they get?

The team was winning before they arrived, wasn't it?" Tarly gave a bland, confident smile. "Do you get the point of view, Christy?"

Christy nodded.

"And do you think this York will make the mistake of trying to teach us anything?"

Instead of answering, Christy shuffled one foot on the porch floor.   "I heard something——"

"What?"

"I—— Well, I don't know how you'll take it. It won't be what I say or think but what I heard."

"Where did you hear this?"

"At the *Argus* office."

"Tell it to me and don't stand there yammering. If it's something important I ought to know it."

"All right, but remember—— Oh, all right. I was talking to one of the *Argus* reporters who knew this York out west. He told me York was poison."

"What kind of poison?" Tarly asked sharply.

"You know, tough. No nonsense and no maybe-I-won't and maybe-I-will. When he gives you an order it's an order, and if you don't do as he says he bears down."

"Why do you say 'You,' Christy? Do you mean me?"

"Of course not. I was speaking generally."

Tarly's eyes became narrow slits again. "Of course," he said softly, "you're not warning me?"

The editor, brick-red, began to stammer. "I—I told you it would be only what—what somebody else said——"

One of Tarly's hands made a benevolent gesture. "I know. You've talked to some blah-blah artist down at the *Argus* and let yourself be stampeded. Leave all this to me. You get away to your uncle's farm early and get back early."

Christy, relieved, departed. After he was gone Tarly picked up the newspaper and read the story again.

"Tough!" he said.

He stood up and, with his head thrown back, stretched his fine, young body lazily. Presently, with his head back, he smiled up at the porch ceiling.

"Oh, I don't know. If it comes to a pinch I think Tarly Ball might prove to be a tough baby himself."

2

The New Coach Arrives

ONE boy, at least, obeyed Tarly Ball on the matter of punctuality. Christy Lee went off to his uncle's farm early in June and was home again by the twentieth of the month.

When he left he was pale, soft, flabby. He turned brown, and hard, and trim. Seventeen days of outdoor life had made him over, and Tarly nodded approvingly.

Here, the captain thought, was something to work with. The plan to mold Christy to his liking and make him a finished end had become an obsession. Christy was to become the jewel of his crown this final year at Mountain High.

It was hard, he told himself, to make a team out of nothing. Yet he had accomplished the miracle. And yet he had brains enough to know that, after a

48

certain point is reached, a team travels on momentum. One man bears another man along; spirits unite and fuse. Taking an individual piece of clay and molding it to your will and purpose was a more difficult, a more ambitious, task. And because it was more difficult, because its accomplishment would mark him definitely as a builder and a creator, it challenged him and quickened his fighting blood.

"My uncle wanted me to stay another week," Christy told him. "I was tempted to stay there."

"Why?"

"Oh, I thought another toughening-up week around the farm——"

Tarly shook a decided head. "Would have meant one less week of football practice. You haven't played the game in three years. Three years is a long time. You have a long distance to travel and a whole lot to learn."

"I've been wondering about that," said Christy.

"About what?"

"About being out three years."

"Forget it," said Tarly. "I'm teaching you." He said it largely, as though there was nothing in the

whole compass of football that was impossible to
him.

That afternoon saw the beginning of a one-man
school of football that was to turn out a polished,
finished end in eight weeks. Carpenters had come to
the school to do some necessary repair work, and
the school janitor had to be there every day. Tarly
talked himself into the locker-room, selected old
football equipment, and brought Christy a uniform
and pads. That afternoon he led the way to a field
on the outskirts of the town.

"Chris, you're in for some punishment. Football
isn't a parlor game—not the way I've taught it
at Mountain High. Football is a game of fight.
Ready?"

Christy said he was ready.

Tarly, down on one knee, spun the pig-skin across
the rough, uneven ground. "Fall on it," he barked.

Christy ran forward, gauged the tumbling ball,
went down in an awkward plunge and grunted hol-
lowly. He had plumped down upon the football
on his stomach and the wind had been knocked out
of him. In sick distress he rolled over on his side.

After a moment his head cleared and he looked up. Tarly Ball stood there frowning down at him.

"Holy cow; that's not the way. Did anybody tell you you were doing a swan dive? Is that the way you went after a loose ball when you were out trying for the team?"

Christy sat up. He still lacked wind enough to speak.

"No wonder you didn't make the scrub. Don't fall on top of the ball. Take it a little to the side. Bring up your knees. Pocket it so that it can't get away; hug it against your stomach and bottle it with your arms and your legs. Of course, if there's a mad scramble you roll over after you have it safe and cover so nobody can snatch it away. What were you trying to do? See if you could hit it dead center and bounce?"

Christy spoke weakly. "How was I to know? Suppose you show me how to do it."

The captain demonstrated, eeling around the ball with practiced ease and skill. He sprang to his feet.

"Get it?"

"Y——yes," Christy said doubtfully.

"All right; let me see you do it."

"Wait a minute," Christy pleaded. "Wait until I get back my wind."

"Do you think a play will stop until you get back your wind? Up on your toes."

At the end of a pain-racked hour Tarly called a halt. The editor sank down upon the ground and rubbed his sides gingerly. It seemed to him that every muscle in his body ached cruelly.

"Gosh!" he sighed dolefully.

"What's the matter?" Tarly asked as though surprised.

"I'm sore all over."

"You'll be a lot sorer before you're through," Tarly said cheerfully. "You've had only one hour of it." It didn't dawn upon the captain that, though the squad practiced for two hours each day, the work was spread out among a great many men. Christy was taking his practice in a concentrated dose. "Up on your feet; pound dirt. Once around the lot. Make it fast and no cutting the corners."

Christy protested. "Gosh, Tarly——"

"So you can't go once around the lot?" Tarly

asked witheringly. "You're tired! What do you
think happens to a man in a game? Do you think
the linesmen bring him out a pillow between plays?
Don't you know that men on the team have to
grit their teeth and keep on when their feet are
lead?" The captain strode away. "I made a mistake
about you, Christy. You don't want to be a football man."

As he swung the first corner he sent a sidelong
glance back across his shoulder. A human form ran
heavily about the lot. He quickened his pace.
Christy had to run an additional two blocks to overtake him. The boy was panting.

"I——I did——it——Tarly."

"After an argument," Tarly said coldly.

"I wasn't——arguing. I——was tired——and for
a few minutes——"

"Oh! I suppose you think a game can stop for
a few minutes while a player gets over being tired?"

"But——"

"There's no buts, Christy. Now that we're at
it we might just as well understand each other. I
can't make you an end unless you want to be an

end. If you want to be an end hard enough, you won't let anything stop you. Did I let anything stop me being the best football man at Mountain? I didn't order you around that lot for pastime. An end must have legs—strong, fast legs. How is he going to develop them unless he uses them? And let me tell you another thing—there are to be no more of these arguments. I'm running this show. If you're going to stay with me you're going to do what you're told."

After that Christy Lee obeyed all the captain's orders without questioning or objecting.

More and more, as the days passed, Tarly became absorbed in this experiment of making something out of nothing. Walking to and from the practice he lectured a rapt pupil out of the richness of his experience. He warned Christy that, above all other considerations, the first duty of an end on defense, is never to let the play outflank him.

"You run it in toward the center, Christy, or else you stay on its tail and keep forcing it out toward the sideline. If you force it to cut in, somebody'll be there to bring it down. If you keep it running toward the sideline, somebody from the secondary will be along to stop it from getting through. Once you're outflanked the runner can make a long gain around the wings. But so long as you keep the man with the ball from going around you they can't get much distance. They may run *across* the field, but they won't get *down* the field toward your line."

"Suppose they do get past the end?"

"They shouldn't if you play your game."

"But suppose they do?"

"If they get around you too often," Tarly snapped, "there'll be somebody else out there playing end."

And thus Christy was given to understand that, though Tarly might make him an end, he himself would write the answer to whether or not he stayed on the team.

On other days the captain opened the door to the secrets of blocking—the art of dodging, feinting, and the use of hands, arms and shoulders. He told Christy that, though an end should go down fast under punts, he should never dash headlong into the man who had made the catch.

"That's the easiest way to have him sidestep you and get away," Tarly warned.

"But I've got to get him," Christy argued.

"Of course. Did I say you didn't? But if you come in like a wild bull and he steps one step to the side, you can't alter your course. Slow a little as you near him. Have yourself in hand so that you can shift if necessary. As soon as you have him where he can't get away, nail him. Don't take him against your shoulder; take him with your chest. When you take him against your chest and bring up your weight, he falls back, not forward. When you take him with your shoulder you risk a broken collar-bone."

"When am I to get tackle practice?"

"We'll start that tomorrow."

After that Tarly played the part of a live tackling-dummy. He ran with the ball and Christy went for him. There were times the captain would be able to dodge; there were times a straight arm would catch Christy flush and bowl him over. But more often Tarly went down. He insisted on hard

tackling. He submitted to being tackled until hips
and thighs ached and began to get raw. He threw
spirals and flat passes until Christy could catch a
forward pass from any angle. Toward the middle
of August he drew a long, slow breath of content-
ment.

"You'll do," he said.

"Honest?" Christy cried.

"I said so, didn't I? I promised I'd turn you into
an end and I've kept my word. When practice
starts next month you'll have an edge on any man
out to play the end of the line."

"Are we all through?" Christy asked hopefully.
Despite the lure of making the team and sporting
a lettered sweater through his final year he had
found this sweating toil under a summer sun hard,
laborious and painful.

"We are not. Do you want to forget all you've
learned? You have to stay with the game if you
want to be good. We'll go right on, about twice a
week. We'll make it a little softer."

Christy said: "Suppose this fellow York should
get the idea that I'm not so hot?"

Tarly's eyes closed to slits as they did when he was angered and aroused. "Well?"

"I mean—— He'll be the coach——"

"Leave that to me," said Tarly.

That night, coming into the Candy Cave for an ice cream soda, he walked into a group of Mountain High football men and into a sudden, abrupt silence. His bold eyes swept over the embarrassed group in swift, alert appraisal.

"Anything I shouldn't hear?" he asked. "No little business of sharpening up a knife for papa?"

Ben Parks flushed. "You ought to know it wouldn't be anything like that."

"If you want to know," McNichol, the quarter-back told him casually, "we were speaking about this man York."

"What York?"

Somebody snickered.

"Oh!" Tarly climbed upon a stool. "You mean this man who's coming here to show us how to win football games."

At that there was a general laugh of derision.

Tarly decided that his words had been pure genius. If the squad had set out to build Basil York a hand-made halo his deft, little dig would promptly bring the business to a halt. After all, it was wise to remind them they were a winning outfit without Mr. York.

And yet the incident disturbed him. In the secret recesses of his mind he had thought of York often and had tried to picture what the man might be. He had had one season of undisputed authority and the taste of kingship had been good. There was no disguising the fact that this man York might be a threat. After all, a coach is a coach, and when the school authorities give him power he has a weapon. If York were going to try to set up his own kingdom, and drive through it with a whip——

Tarly's eyes smouldered. He fell back upon a thought that had consoled him these past few weeks. Basil! Basil York! Somehow, the name did not click. It didn't sound as though it might belong to a tough egg. It didn't paint mental pictures the way a name like "Cannonball" Ball did.

And suddenly Tarly laughed and was at ease.

Probably this Basil York would prove to be another Mr. Cudleigh. Not that the captain shrank
from fighting for the kingdom he had created.
Wasn't he the fighting captain of a fighting team?
But he preferred to be able to go along and give his
whole mind to his kingdom and not half of it to
someone who might try to steal his crown.

Mid-August scorched, and practice—even so little
as a twice-a-week practice—proved to be torture
when one was encumbered with moleskins and
jersey.

And yet, because it was not in his nature to quit
or to seek the easy way, he drove along with the
exhausting work and carried a wilted Christy with
him. The last Saturday of the month saw them going through the routine of the final practice session.
He flipped a final pass, a long diagonal shot, and
watched Christy snipe it out of the air on a dead
run. He began to applaud. It seemed to him to be
an omen, a happy augury of good fortune to come.
Well, he was glad the work was over. A rest
wouldn't hurt him; he did not want to start the
season stale. Now he could give careful, undisturbed

thought to the season that was right around the corner.

Walking home from the vacant lot he began to make plans. A man named York was far, far from his thoughts.

He'd start practice on September 8. Right from the start he'd put Christy Lee into the line and get him used to the feel of the other players. With McNichol heaving and Christy catching the ball far down the field, they ought to be able to build up a beautiful forward passing game that would make any opposing team open up. How fast he would develop the team would depend a lot upon how fast the men came along. By the time the first game was played he ought to have a clear, bird's-eye view of the entire season.

He turned in from the wide, friendly street of maples and strode along the flower-bordered walk toward the house. A man arose from a wicker chair on the porch.

"Are you Tarly Ball?"

"Yes, sir."

"Your mother told me to wait, that you'd be

along. Getting into shape early, aren't you? How hot was it out there in the sun today, around 102?"

Tarly laughed. "Not quite as bad as that." He thought he ought to offer some explanation so that he would not look foolish to this stranger who evidently knew something about football. "I had a man to look over. He hasn't played the game very long so I've been giving him an early start."

"I was sure you knew better. My name's York. You and I are going to see a lot of each other. It seemed a good idea to come around and get acquainted."

Tarly had a momentary feeling of chagrin that he had gone to the bother of an explanation. It put him, in a sense, on the defensive. But how should he have known that this was Basil York? A coach, coming to confer with a captain before the opening of the football season, was something unique in the history of Mountain High. He shook hands limply and tried, in his sudden agitation, to find something to say.

But if his tongue was momentarily helpless, his eyes were hot and critical. His appraisal went over the visitor with a sharp scrutiny that missed no detail. About thirty. Thick and powerful shoulders; a waist small and trim. No question about it, a man. And then the taking-stock glance went up to hair as fiery red as his own and to eyes that were strangely cool and disconcerting.

"When did you get in?" Tarly asked.

"Last night. I had to hunt around to find a house and that took almost all the day. Finished about three-quarters of an hour ago, walked over here and sat down to wait."

"I don't suppose you know very much about us?" Tarly was all set to tell the story of Christy Lee. He wanted to get that story in quickly. It had dawned on him that it might have been a mistake to tell this man that Christy had played very little.

York smiled. "I might surprise you if I told you how much I know about the team."

Tarly was disconcerted.

"As a matter of fact this appointment was in the air a year ago. I took a chance and ran down from my home and saw the game with Valley last November."

"We took them nicely," Tarly boasted.

"Nicely," Basil York agreed. "Here and there were spots where you threw away opportunities and might have done better. However, I suppose, after a game is over, it is always easy to be a good second-guesser. Your quarterback—— What's his name?"

"McNichol."

"Yes; McNichol. I thought he showed lapses of judgment in calling forward passes."

"I told him that," Tarly said quickly. "You have to be a bit careful with Mac. He's not the type that stands up well under criticism. Touchy, you know."

York nodded as though he, too, had met touchy personalities in his day.

Tarly felt better. The impression grew on him that he and this new coach from out of the west were going to get on together famously.

"Most of the time," York said, "when you carried the ball, you hit the right side of the line. Why?"

Tarly explained. "I get off to a bit faster start

when I hit to the right. Speed meant a lot to us. We weren't any too heavy."

"That's a good reason. But the left side of the Valley line was the weaker side; they showed it in three or four ways. That side should have been pounded consistently. But then, you won. There's no better answer than that." The man was smiling again. "I suppose no two persons ever see a game eye to eye."

Tarly met that smile with an abrupt frown. His ideas about getting on together began to change. What was this, criticism?

"I've been looking over this year's schedule," Basil York went on. "It seems to me——"

"Where did you get the schedule?" Tarly broke in, astounded.

"I wrote to the *Argus*. I knew that they'd have published it sometime during the spring."

Tarly said with an attempt at cool control: "Don't you think you should have written to me?"

"I was a little afraid you might come to the conclusion I was taking over control prematurely."

That word "control" had an ugly sound. Al-

110

most a sinister sound. Tarly, acutely resentful now, saw his chance to fire a telling shot and promptly fired it.

"Aren't you doing that now?" he demanded.

"Frankly," York said with a disarming smile, "I am. Officially, I don't take over my duties here until September 7. But you and I have so much in common, our interests are so identical, I thought we could, perhaps, save some valuable time if I waited over this afternoon for a preliminary conference."

Tarly knew there was no objection he could make to that. It came to him, with a sense of uneasiness, that this York might be one of those very clever gentlemen and that it might be necessary for him to play clever, too. Sound strategy dictated that he play a watchful game and wait to see what would happen.

"What were you going to say about the schedule?" he asked.

"You're not tied up with some of the schools you play early in the season, are you?"

"In what way?"

"I mean on agreements to meet them annually for a definite number of years?"

The captain shook his head.

"That's good. So often schools sign these long agreements and then live to regret them. I never did care for this idea of picking out a lot of weak-sister opponents during September and October."

Tarly bristled. What was this, a dig that Mountain High wasn't the fourteen-carat fighting team it had been pictured in song and legend?

"We've never picked out a lot of cripples for the sake of piling up a record," he said with heat.

The coach still smiled. "Come, Tarly; we don't want to start by misunderstanding one another. I didn't mean that."

"What did you mean?"

"I thought perhaps those teams went on your schedule years ago and stayed there through force of habit. I've run into incidents like that. But these early season victories against a weak opposition sometimes accustom a team to winning too easily. Every game should teach something; every game should be a little harder assignment than the last.

The team should be able to acquire its necessary edge by battling a strong scrub."

"Suppose there isn't a strong scrub?"

"Of course, that's a problem, isn't it? There always should be a strong scrub. Where are the players for next year and the year after coming from if not from the scrub? Practically all of the men who were first-string players last season graduate next June. At least, so I understand. What then?"

Oh! So Mr. Basil York had begun to criticize, had he? Starting to show that he was a tough egg. Captain Tarly Ball balanced lightly on his toes.

"It just happens," he said lightly, "that there isn't what you might call a strong scrub. Fairly good, but not strong. We never have had a strong scrub."

"That," York smiled, "is one of the reasons I came here today—so I could get a line-up. You and I will have to put our heads together and change this system that gives Mountain a tissue-paper scrub. I'm sure we can do it if we go after it."

Once more that smile left Tarly impotent. What could you do to a coach—how could you put a chip on your shoulder and get tough—if he invited you in to run a plan?

"There's another point we may as well settle, Tarly. About getting practice under way——"

"I've already decided on that," said Tarly.

The man was silent a moment. He seemed lost in thought. "What had you decided?"

"I've already decided to call the team together on September 8. School opens on the seventh."

"Ordinarily," York commented, "that would be a good idea."

Every part of Tarly went sharp with suspicion. That "ordinarily" sounded like another objection.

"As a rule," York went on, "I am opposed to bringing a team together before school starts. But I'm new here and that's a handicap. I'd like a chance to get to know the men. Within two more weeks the weather will begin to cool a little; the squad would probably look upon a little football as good fun and be keen for it. We can get in a week of preliminary work and have our conditioning out of the way. How about the boys? Many of them out of town on vacation by early September?"

"I think they'll all be home by the end of this month. But——"

"That's better than I dared hope for." Again that smile that Tarly was beginning to find maddening. "You know them all; I know none of them. Will you pass the word around and tell them to report at the high school field at two o'clock on the afternoon of September 1?"

Tarly, his mouth open to make heated protest, was halted abruptly by another question from York.

"You have a man—I didn't see much of him—but I think his name is Macy. Am I right?"

"What about him?" Tarly asked, his eyes narrowed.

"Don't forget to have him on hand. He has possibilities. If I remember rightly he played through the last three or four minutes of the Valley game."

Tarly froze. So it was going to be Joe Macy, too!

"He wouldn't have gotten into the game, then," the captain snapped, "only Ben Parks hurt his knee."

"After watching him through a play or two I wondered why he hadn't come in earlier. What was the matter, did you hold him out because of an old injury?"

"I held him out because I didn't want him."

"Why?"

"I didn't like his work. He's one of those fellows who's a little too fond of himself."

York's lips twitched. A dragon fly hovered outside the porch its wings all splendid color in the rays of the declining sun.

"That never does help a man," the coach said. After a moment he picked up his hat. "Nevertheless, I think there's the makings of a real football man in Macy."

Tarly's lips had set. "That's where you and I differ. I never thought much of him."

"Why?"

"I told you before."

"Sorry. You merely said you didn't like his work. I'm asking you what's wrong with his work?"

"He can't make the grade."

"I'm sorry to hear that," York said pleasantly. "I thought he showed all the ear-marks of a comer. If you're right in your opinion I seem to be ignorant of what it takes to make the grade."

"Evidently you are."

The dragon-fly made a dart and was gone. Tarly said a satisfied, inward: "How do you like that, Mr. York?" and watched the man absently fleck a speck of dust from the ribbon of his Panama.

"There's never any telling," York said, unperturbed. "I suppose we might set that down as one more reason why it should be advantageous for us to get an early start."

Tarly was mystified. "What is?"

"This question of who can make the grade and who can't. In other words, undiscovered talent. There may be a few more rough diamonds as promising as Macy hidden away. September 1, at two o'clock. And make sure that word of the practice gets to Macy." The coach moved toward the steps.

A higher shade of red than was customary had crept into Tarly's ruddy cheeks. Swaying from the hips, walking lightly and dangerously on his toes, he went forward a stride and partly blocked the porch steps.

"About this early practice, Mr. York. Let's come to an agreement. I don't think we have that settled yet."

"No?" drawling.

"No," tartly.

"My mistake. I thought everything was understood."

"Not by a long shot. We've never before found it necessary to start practice before the opening of school." If the work started with an innovation the squad would see York's hand at once. "Personally, I don't see the sense of it. I don't see why we must do what we have never done before."

The smile was gone from York's face and he looked serious and stern. "There will probably be a lot of things down at the field this year that were never done before."

"Such as?"

"Such as practice before school opens."

The fighting blood of Tarly Ball smoked. So this was what Christy Lee meant by bearing down, was it? A tough guy! He cocked his head to one side.

"I wouldn't be so sure about that. So far as practice that early is concerned, we've gotten along very well without it. You read the newspapers, don't you? The sports writers have been saying that we're one of the best teams——"

"Do you let the sports writers run football here?"

The red in Tarly's cheeks became painful. "We don't let anybody run football here. But when reporters who ought to know say that we have one of the best teams——"

"That's splendid, isn't it?" the coach drawled. "I've known cases where sports writers have learnedly discussed a team and showed signs of really not knowing what they were talking about. But suppose we try to go beyond 'one of the best teams.' Let's make this not one of the best teams but the *best* team."

"That's something I've already planned."

York nodded in contemplation, and his eyes looked straight into the captain's. And the famous bold, fighting eyes of Tarly Ball fell rebelliously.

"You had more or less of a free hand with the team for several years, didn't you?" the coach asked.

"What do you mean by that?"

"I merely asked."

"I made a success of it, didn't I?"

"All things considered," York admitted seriously, "you made quite a success of it. Well, let the men know."

"But I tell you——"

"Growing cooler, isn't it?" York had stepped around the boy and was halfway down the porch steps.

"But look here——"

"September 1, at two o'clock." York smiled pleasantly.

But the smile touched only his lips and did not show in his eyes. Tarly, helpless, had that same feeling of furious impotence.

"September 1, at two o'clock," the man said again, and was gone.

CHAPTER
3

York Takes Command

FOR a bad, smouldering hour Tarly Ball thought of saying nothing to the team about September 1.

In his imagination he pictured York arriving at the field and finding nobody there and waiting around for players who did not come. That would show the new coach that he couldn't walk right into an established kingdom and begin to pull things around.

But as Tarly's blood cooled it dawned upon him regretfully, that the plan simply wouldn't work. It offered him nothing in the way of permanent gain. Though he was convinced that it was only a question of time before he and York came to an open clash and a fight for supremacy, he saw no reason for fighting when, even though he won, the victory would be transient and hollow. For if the team did not appear on September 1 York would probably visit the players one by one and issue his commands. The practice session to which Tarly objected would be delayed only one day at the most.

And so, on the morrow, he notified the team.

Though rebellion raged in his heart he allowed no sign of dissatisfaction to creep into his voice. For one thing he did not want the players to suspect that this was something to which he objected but which he was powerless to stop. For another, it seemed a wiser plan to wait and to watch. Let this man York dig himself a nice, deep pit. When the pit became deep enough and broad enough there should be no trouble about pitching the coach into it and being done with meddling forever.

He went to Christy Lee to give his protege the practice call. Christy, however, had news of his own.

"York was in town yesterday, wasn't he?"

Tarly was staggered. "How did you know that?"

"One of the men at the *Argus* told me—you

know, that reporter who had met York out west. He ran into him."

"York and I wanted to keep the visit quiet," Tarly said. "We're going to start practice on September 1."

"Why so early?"

"Look here, do you think York has forced this on me?"

"I didn't say that; I only asked."

"You'll do better if you follow orders and ask less questions. York and I thought it best to advance the date a week. He doesn't know the gang and it gives him a chance to size them up."

"But you could tell him——"

"Oh, you know how it is with a new man. He knows everybody'll be watching him. He doesn't want to have them see him leaning too much on the captain."

"A different sort of coach than Mr. Cudleigh, isn't he?"

"For a while," Tarly said. He could not understand why he had allowed the man to ride him down. Probably he had been startled and not up to his best. From this point on, though, York wouldn't find things quite so easy to manage—not if, by managing, he was going to cut up a whole list of new capers.

Christy said: "Are you sure I'm all right, Tarly?"

"Holy cow, will you stop your moaning? Who's been training you? What have I been training you for? Haven't I made the Mountain High team what it is? Don't you think I know what a man needs to make the team?"

The editor's doubts were lulled.

Joe Macy took the tidings with a quiet nod and asked the same question that had been framed by Christy. "Early for practice, isn't it?"

"You starting to question orders given by York and me?" Tarly demanded. If Christy knew York had been in town others would have the information, too. Better to bring in York's name himself than have to make embarrassing explanations.

"If I had any questions to raise," Joe said coolly, "I'd wait until York got here."

There was a slap in that, and Tarly flushed.

Covertly he studied the other boy with a puzzled frown. So this was the man York thought Mountain High was wasting! The captain shook his head—the whole thing was a riddle.

Had his eyes traveled up to Macy's face he might have seen something that would have given him pause. For on Macy's face was the look of one who sees at last the promise of a hope long deferred.

"I'll be there," was all the scrub back said.

York had marked the hour for two o'clock. At half-past one, thirty-three boys, dressed and nervous, moved restlessly about the high school gym gripped by that uneasy constraint that seizes young players about to come face to face for the first time with unknown authority. The thirty-fourth, in the person of Tarly Ball, strolled in at a quarter to two. Through a window he could see a broad-shouldered, slim-waisted figure looking over the field. Whistling, the captain got into uniform and looked about him.

"Met York yet?"

None of them had. York, it appeared, had been on the field when the first player reached the gym.

"Why don't you go out? Afraid of him?"

"You met him," came in Joe Macy's clipped tones. "Is he a man to be afraid of?"

Tarly gave the scrub back a venomous glance.

"We were waiting for you," said Parks.

Tarly warmed. That was the way to have your men—waiting for you. He gave them a grin.

"All right, gang. Let's see how hard he bites." He led the way. York, in his football togs, was a fine stalwart man. There was about him an atmosphere of vitality and controlled strength that Mr. Cudleigh, buried in his studies and his writings, had sadly lacked. He stood on the thirty-yard line with a football in his hands. As the squad approached he dropped the ball, his leg swung as though on oiled hinges, there was a solid plunk. The football, tumbling end over end, sailed high into the air and dropped clean and true between the goal posts and above the bar.

"That's kicking," a voice breathed.

"Scenery," Tarly muttered under his breath. "Putting on a show for the audience."

But in the depth of his heart he wished he could

punt as the coach had punted. It had been a good show.

York, smiling the smile that the captain had found maddening, met the squad near the sideline.

"Everybody here, Tarly?"

"Everybody."

"I don't think we need to waste any time going through introductions. There are so many of you, I wouldn't be able to remember all your names. Anyway, we'll manage to get very well acquainted as we go along. That's one of the things I like about football—it binds men together in work and in effort and they come to have a close understanding of each other. A week from now I'll know which of you are any good and you'll probably have come to a rather definite conclusion as to whether I am any good."

"That was a honey of a kick," said Elliott, one of the ends.

Tarly gave Elliott a bland stare. Sucking around? Well, that wouldn't mean anything. Elliott was the man, in his opinion, whose place Christy Lee was to take at right end.

"Oh, that!" York laughed. "Anybody can kick on a deserted field. It's rather a different story when a couple of wolves break through and come tearing down to block. Tarly and I have decided that a fighting team tells only half the story; if you're going to build for the future you have to have a good, fighting scrub. He tells me conditions haven't been right for the building of a bull-dog scrub before. We're going to try to change that."

WE! Tarly bit his lips and watched the men narrowly. The "we" was better than he had expected.

"I want every man to understand this and I want him to understand it clearly. The fact that he plays on the scrub today is no guarantee or pledge of where he plays tomorrow. No first-string man is married to his job. No man on this team has won a job by what he has shown in other seasons. That may sound hard, but it is just. If some player surpasses him, that player should have his place. He holds it only as long as he can prove title to it. Football is, and always has been, a survival of the fittest. While it may be hard to drop a veteran, it would be as hard to hold back a man coming along with a rush. After all, that veteran displaced somebody else. The rule gave him his chance and gave him his place; he has no complaint if the same rule waves him aside in favor of a better player."

Oh! So it had become "I." "I want it understood." Tarly bit his lips harder.

"When a man plays scrub it means he's a second-string man, doesn't it?" Joe Macy asked.

York gave him a smile. "I think I remember you. Your name Macy?"

"Yes, sir."

"Where did you get that idea?"

Macy's eyes went obliquely toward the captain. "You sort of get ideas," he answered.

This time York's smile broadened and took in the entire group. "Let me answer that this way. When I was at college——"

"What college?" Joe Macy asked.

"Allwater. You've probably never heard of it. What some folks call a 'fresh-water college.' When I was at college we had a man who worked on the scrub until the middle of his last season.

Then he went to the 'Varsity.' That had been his intended place from the start, but a wise coach knew he was weak on defensive play. So he got defensive play as only a scrub man gets it. Defensive play was beaten into him. As a result, when he came over to the 'Varsity' he became one of the greatest linesmen in Allwater history. Playing on the scrub merely means that Mountain can use you there to the best advantage at that particular time. Not tomorrow. Not next week or next month. Only that day, that particular time. Everybody get that?"

A chorus came from the group. "Yes, sir."

"All right, then. Ends down the field, centers and quarters to the middle, backfield men follow me."

There was nothing for Captain Tarly Ball to do but to go along with the other backs. It was the first practice session in three years in which he had not given the orders. The thought stuck hard in his throat and gave him the sensation that he was choking.

That first day went as first days go whenever

football teams gather for practice—handling the ball, falling on the ball, kicking and passing. Ben Parks, the first man to kick, swung his right leg with all his strength. The ball shot off at a tangent. Tarly, following the course of the ball, chuckled. He wasn't a York, but wait until his turn came. He'd show them distance.

But to his surprise York was out among the backs waving his hands in the signal that the work was to halt.

"Who kicked that ball?"

"I did," Parks answered.

"What's your name?"

"Ben Parks."

"That's not the way to kick your first day out. Among other unfortunate circumstances you might tear a muscle. Simply drop the ball and swing your foot to meet it. Nobody's worrying about distance now. That will come later. Now we want correct form. If you get that you can be taught all the rest easily. Is that clear?"

The backfield men nodded that the instruction had been perfectly clear.

"This way," said York. He dropped a ball and lifted it lazily. And yet, lazy as the kick was, the ball traveled high and far.

"That's distance," Macy commented.

"Nothing but form. Distance is the short end of the story. What good is distance if you never know where the ball is going when it leaves your foot? If you're about midfield and kicking for a corner it makes a twenty-yard difference whether you hit in around the corner or go over the line. The man whose form is bad only gets off an occasionally accurate kick. We want every man to have the confidence of the other ten. That includes the kicker. That's what makes for team-work. Try that kick again, and——"

Abruptly York stopped talking, swung about, and was off down the field toward the linesmen. Tarly saw him descend upon a player chasing a ball. Voices came back to the captain:

"You! You, over there! The man who just dropped that pass. What's your name?"

"Lee, sir—Christy Lee."

"How long have you been playing football?"

"Not very long."

"I thought not. Never make a joke of practice. Practice is a preparation for what you have to do in a game, and you'll come pretty close to doing in those games what you do in practice. Squeeze the ball. After a time it will become such a habit that you'll always squeeze the ball unconsciously. Here! Somebody throw this man a pass. Squeeze it, Lee."

The ball came hurtling through the air, traveling on its axis. Christy, anxious now, froze to the pigskin and showed that Tarly's coaching had not been in vain.

"That's the way to do it, old man. Never any other way." York patted the editor's shoulder. And all at once the sting was gone from the criticism.

Tarly burned. Luck had played him a shabby trick. If somebody was fated to blunder badly today, why did it have to be the one man he had coached?

At the end of forty minutes York blew a shrill whistle and the squad came forward from all directions and gathered about him. The man, Tarly thought bitterly, could at least have asked him if he thought the practice had lasted long enough.

"We must be careful not to overdo this," York said crisply. "A wise pound is preferable to an unwise ton. Two o'clock tomorrow. Once around the field and no loafing."

The squad went off at a fast clip. Tarly wondered if the coach expected him to leg along after the others. He spread his feet apart and anchored.

"Been getting much exercise during the summer?" York asked. "Baseball, tennis, swimming?"

The captain saw what was coming and was powerless. He couldn't tell York he had selected one of the ends weeks ago, that he had been giving Christy an hour of football almost every day. Certainly not after the maddening exhibition Christy had given that afternoon. He shook his head.

"Mountain's going to need you, Tarly, and that means you'll have to be in shape."

Still the captain stood with his legs spread. Would York actually order him to take the work of the others?

"You'd better cut after them. That bit of running is good stuff for the wind and the legs."

Tarly, a hot lump of exasperation burning his throat, trotted away after the others.

York was stationed at the gymnasium door as the crowd passed inside. Joe Macy, running easily and without effort, was almost the last man. The coach tapped him on the shoulder.

"You have a good football stride, Macy. Your knees come up high. How do you stand up? Injure easily through a season?"

Joe shook his head. "An odd bruise. I've never really been hurt."

"Good! I like tough-fibred men. You throw a nice flat pass; a little heavy; I'll have to show you the trick of throwing a light ball. Makes the job of the man on the receiving end a little easier. I saw you in the last Valley game. How often did you get into the game last season?"

"That was my only game."

York remembered. Tarly had told him the Valley game marked Joe's only appearance of the year. He nodded thoughtfully. "How long have you been with the scrub?"

"Three years."

"That's a long time, Macy. What are you, a senior?"

"Yes, sir."

"This is your last chance."

Joe Macy said nothing.

"I'm here to be shown," York said quietly. "If you have anything to show—— Well, it's up to you."

Tarly, seeing the two together, came up the field at a fast pace. But when he arrived outside the gym entrance Macy had disappeared inside and York was passing through the door. What was the coach doing, playing up to Macy already? If York had any idea he was going to jam a lot of hand-picked favorites into the line-up—— He saw Christy and took out his spleen upon the editor.

"You picked out a fine day to play a dumb trick, didn't you? Do you realize how that makes me look?"

Christy looked unhappy. "One balled up play shouldn't kill a man off for the season. Everybody slips."

"You don't know this man York."

Christy became alarmed. "You mean he's tough?"

Tarly awoke to the fact that he had already said the wrong thing. "I mean he may get ideas. What's the use of getting me tangled up with him if it can be avoided? There'll be plenty of time to put him in his place."

But before another week was out the captain had a panicky feeling that putting the smiling Mr. York in his place was a job that might already have slipped beyond him.

If he had fought the battle out that first day on the porch—— But he hadn't, and since then he had been steadily giving ground bit by bit. Suddenly the grand total of all he had surrendered appalled him. York had always smiled, and listened, and explained. Always beneath that smile, though, there had been unbending steel. And Tarly, baffled and furious, had found himself unable to penetrate the armor of the man's will.

All at once he knew the full truth. The good old days were gone. A little here and a little there, and the trick had been done. One by one the conditions and traditions he had established had been changed or set aside. And the greatest change had come in the hour set for the practice.

Under Mr. Cudleigh the hour had always been pleasantly elastic. Tarly did not like the system; but, finding himself unable to change it, he had allowed it to run on. He still held to his original thought that football was not a jail run on a rigid schedule.

York had different ideas. Two o'clock was two o'clock. Once the coach issued a warning, cloaking it with a smile.

"It isn't fair, men," he said, "to have some players come here early and have to wait around in idleness until other players arrive. First thing we know the early men will decide there is no reason to come early; that means the late-comers will set the pace. If you have a train to catch you have to be at the station on time. This is the Mountain Express. We're going places. I want every man here when the train pulls out each day."

That first warning worked very little change. The second warning was sharper.

"A man who can't get to the field on time is a man who can't be depended upon to do anything on time. If he's a linesman he opens holes late. If he's a back carrying the ball he gets to the holes late. This team has no place for the professional delayer."

The next day Parks emerged from the gym after the squad had got down to business. Unconcerned, he trotted across the field and joined the backs, drawing on his headguard as he ran.

York halted the practice. "What are you doing here, Parks?"

"I came out to practice."

"Did you? Practice started fifteen minutes ago. Get over there beyond the sideline and keep out of the way of men who take their work seriously."

Parks, not knowing quite what to make of this, hesitated.

"On your way," York said sharply.

A sullen, scowling backfield man retreated beyond the sideline and cast Tarly a mute appeal for aid. No aid was forthcoming from the old, unquestioned leader.

"What's the idea?" Parks demanded of the captain when the practice was over. "Who's boss around here?"

Tarly stalled for time. "Who do you think is boss?"

"By the looks of things, York is boss. If he isn't you're certainly letting him get away with murder."

Tarly made a weak stab at denial. "I'm waiting until he goes a little too far."

"Too far?" Parks gave a hollow laugh. "What do you call too far? You must be a glutton for punishment."

Tarly's red-haired temper flared. "Would you like to enjoy a permanent station on the sideline?"

The next moment he knew he had made another serious mistake. Ben Parks was his friend. Today Parks had looked to him for leadership; Parks was one of his old teammates. Events had certainly arrived at a sorry pass when he bowed his head to the iron of York's rule and quarreled with those who would give him loyalty.

Another upset came on the morrow. Tarly had always taught his men to try to smear and scatter the interference by going into it with a headlong dash and trying to spill it right and left. York insisted, patiently, that a man running interference or smashing interference should never intentionally leave his feet if this could be avoided.

"If you can take out your man and stay on your feet," he said, "it naturally follows that you're still dangerous. You haven't passed out of the play. You're in position to keep on going and perhaps take out another man."

"We were never taught that system," said Parks.

"Who taught you?"

"Tarly," Parks jabbed. The answer was a shot shrewdly calculated to start something.

It started nothing.

"This is a newer system," York explained smoothly. It was a newer football system. But the coach did not tell them how many years since the system had been new.

Other changes followed from day to day. Men were taught to let their whole bodies go limp as they caught a pass or a punt. And again it was Parks who argued.

"That's another system we were never taught, Coach."

York did not make the mistake this time of asking the name of the teacher. He had gauged Parks as a trouble-maker and he would do all in his power to avoid an open breach with the captain.

Parks grunted. The bait had been refused. He asked another question: "If you're limp when you catch a forward pass or a punt, how are you going to get started on a run?"

"You're getting the play backwards and putting the cart before the horse, aren't you?" York asked coolly.

Parks stared.

"Before you can run you must first catch the ball. That's the idea behind this system, isn't it, Tarly?"

Tarly said a slow, reluctant "Yes." The coach's logic was impregnable and left him helpless. There was nothing for him to do but to agree.

Parks gave him a sidelong, sardonic glance.

That glance was wormwood. Accustomed to a free and autocratic hand, the captain found it harder each day to accept his smaller status. A new force overshadowed the field. A man lean and hard, with alert eyes that seemed to be able to see four ways at once, dominated the field and the players.

There were times when he knew York took the trouble to go out of his way to soften some ruling that reversed a previous custom—and that was galling. The bitterness that crept into his fighting blood came, in time, to possess the current of his whole thought. Twice he went to York to protest some change only to find his own arguments deftly turned against him. He always made these protests in private for he feared the effect of a public humiliation. He grew furious at his own ineffectiveness.

"Tarly," said the coach, "surely you don't believe there's anything personal in what I'm doing?"

"How do I know that?"

"Do you mean what you've just said?" There was a quality in the man's voice that the captain had never heard before.

"You're certainly going out of your way to pull my type of play all to pieces," Tarly blurted.

"Do you really believe I go out of my way?"

Tarly was uncomfortably silent. He had a sick conviction that he was talking like a fool. That did not make him feel any better.

"If you do believe that, Tarly, you have less vision than I thought. I pull the old system apart only when necessary. I'm not criticizing anything that happened in the past. Lord, man, can't you realize that I understand what the situation here was? Considering that you had the whole load to carry you did wonders. Frankly, I don't know another high school captain who could have done it. Nevertheless, there's a lot you don't know. If you look at it sensibly, that's only natural. You're only a boy; your experience has been limited; you'd had to pick things up by yourself. With you football is a game; with me it is a profession. That makes a vast difference. If you blunder along and have a poor season—— Well, it's been a poor season and that's all there is to it. If I don't know my business I can't hold my job. Surely you can see that?"

Again the logic was all with York. But Tarly, harassed by the sting of personal failure in that his kingdom had passed from him, was in no mood for logic.

"What difference does it make whether I do or not?" He sulked off toward the gym, and York shook his head and sighed.

There came a day when tentative first and second teams were announced. Parks went to the first team and Joe Macy to his old place on the scrub. Tarly had a moment of satisfaction. Then he had been right about Macy, after all. He had argued the point with York last night. He waited for the list of linesmen. He had argued that, too, and one position had been left open. However, the question was open no longer, for the coach sent Elliott in as right end for the school team and sent Christy Lee to the scrub.

Parks went out to the field at Tarly's heels. "Who picked the teams? You?"

"I had a hand in it. Why?"

Parks shrugged. "I wondered. You promised Christy he'd play end, didn't you?"

Tarly stopped short. "Who told you that?"

"Oh, the whole team knows it. If you wanted Christy why isn't he there?"

"York and I decided to wait a while and let him develop," Tarly said with stiff hauteur.

So Christy had talked! The news of his promise could have come from no one else. And as clearly as he knew that, he also knew that in last night's discussion his had been a minor voice. York had filled the positions and, except in the cases of Macy and Christy, he had approved. He had won his war on Macy—at least temporarily. He had lost on Christy. Suddenly Macy ceased to matter. Where Joe played became a matter of secondary interest. The fate of Christy Lee became his chief interest. The whole team knew he had committed himself to Christy.

Above the head of a player he saw the appealing eyes of the editor and his jaw hardened. Let York do as he wished with Macy, but Christy had to be saved. Christy was his own creation. And besides, he had given his word.

That day there was a blackboard talk on the field

and after that the first and second teams, at different ends of the field, walked through signal drills. When the work was over Tarly waited on the field with the coach.

"I want Christy Lee on the first team," he said abruptly. Somehow, the sentence didn't sound strong enough. "In fact, I insist."

York reached down and plucked a blade of grass. "You promised Christy that, didn't you?"

Tarly went red. Was somebody on the squad playing coach's pet and whispering in the coach's ear? How else could York have come by this information.

"Suppose I did?" he demanded, truculently.

"That was foolish, wasn't it?"

"Why so? I know the men. I knew Elliott. I thought he was better than Elliott."

"You didn't know what Elliott might do this season."

"I knew what he had done in other seasons."

"In what way do you think Christy's better?"

"He's faster. Anybody can see that. The way he can pick a ball out of the air he's a sure bet on the receiving end of a forward pass combination."

York's face was grave. He creased the grass blade and snapped it in the middle.

"Yes; he is faster. I grant you that. Unfortunately, however, a very small percentage of plays are forward pass plays. I'm sorry, but I'm afraid he's where he belongs. We haven't had any actual scrimmage yet, but you watched while I played one man on defense and put two men against him. His weakness was apparent. He doesn't know how to hold off interference. A smart team would find him out the first time they struck at his end. After that he'd be outflanked and bewildered. There'd be a happy parade down the side of the field he was supposed to guard."

Once more Tarly knew York had pierced him with a logic that was not to be confounded. Of course Christy was weak on defense. How could he be anything else? He had had the benefit of only a one-man practice during those weeks of July and August and no man can learn how to handle two or three interferers merely by blocking off one man. But he was sure that Christy would pick up the trick as he had picked up the knack of catching a ball.

"This isn't final?" the captain asked at last.

"Of course not. Nothing is final at this point. How can we tell what man will blossom into brilliance tomorrow? We're experimenting, trying to fit them together so that we can get the best results. There are men on the scrub today who will probably be over with the first team within two weeks."

Tarly told that to the editor of the *Mountain Goat*. He told it with gusto, trying hard to save his reputation as a prophet and to preserve the halo of infallibility with which Christy, in sincere admiration, had invested him. And yet he saw, with a pang, that the end's faith was shaken.

"Maybe I should never have gone into this," Christy said soberly.

"What do you mean?"

"Maybe I should have kept out of football. I wasn't worth a hill of beans three years ago."

"Why talk about three years ago? Three years ago you didn't have me coaching you. Don't you think that makes a difference? Didn't I tell you you were good? Well, didn't I?"

"I know——" Christy's voice trailed off. "Did you notice York watching me the day he was showing us linesmen how to block?"

Tarly shook with rage. Christy and York talking to the same point! Fate at that moment seemed to be a Nemesis slowly pressing him to defeat.

"York was watching everybody, wasn't he?"

Christy looked steadily at some object far up the street. "I won't hold you to that promise, Tarly."

"What does that mean? That you think I can't make good?"

"No. I didn't mean exactly that."

"Oh! Not exactly that. That's rich, that is. Well, let me tell you something, Christy. I'm the one to say whether or not that promise can be kept."

"But—but if sticking to me is going to get you all messed up with York——"

It was an unfortunate speech. It sent the blood into Tarly's head and froze his lips into a thin line.

"York," the captain cried in a passion, "has nothing to do with it. This is my team. The men elected me. I'm in command and what I say goes. Don't forget that. It's my team, and you'll play the day I say you'll play. If you're on the scrub now you're there to get experience."

All at once he saw in Christy Lee's admiring eyes a return of the old, unshaken confidence.

"My team!" he repeated.

A wonder grew upon him. Why, he had lost sight of the fact that it was his team. York was here through an accident of choice; the Board of Education might have selected any one of a dozen other men. But he was the captain because he was the one man the team had unanimously wanted. The picture filled him with a glowing tide of fresh courage and he drew a deep breath.

"I think," he said aloud after Christy had disappeared in the distance, "Mr. York has gone about as far as he's going to go in his song and dance."

4

Rebellion Shows Its Head

AFTER that day a change came over Tarly Ball. His eyes were a constant flame of battle and he walked more lightly on his toes. He was an ax-man looking for a place to sink the ax.

Nor did he hesitate to make a public show of his revolt. Heretofore he had argued for his ideas when he and York were alone, afraid to run the risk of an open defeat before the squad. Now, suddenly, his objections were made boldly and baldly before the team. He stated them clearly, with a hard, cool insolence, his hands on his hips, his body swaying nervously and lightly.

The effect was immediate. A shock of re-awakened interest ran through the squad. He noted this instant reaction and his wounded pride was salved.

"I knew this would come," Parks chuckled. "The old fighting blood is up."

Tarly heard that. The words rang in his ears like sweet music. His heart swelled.

"When," he asked softly, "was the fighting blood ever low?"

Tight little lines of worry began to creep around the corner of the coach's mouth.

And slowly the thought came to Tarly, the more he thought of his conversation with Christy Lee, the longer he thought of Ben Parks' chuckling delight, that many others of the squad were probably dissatisfied with the changed conditions at Mountain High. Had he been less obsessed with his own bitter grievances something in him instinctively loyal would have taken fright. He would have seen, in this menace of dissatisfaction, a ghastly threat of disaster and of ruin.

Now all he saw was a state of mind that might possibly be swung to his advantage and made to produce necessary allies. He had sense enough to realize that he could not fight York alone. Alone he was whipped; but with the backing of the team he could command. He had no doubts. He was convinced that he could get along with York; that, in fact, he did not need the coach. He had led the team to victory before and he could do it again.

Parks walked home with him from the practice—a slow, thoughtful walk. "You talked like the old Tarly today," the back said, and watched the captain narrowly.

Tarly debated. Should he open a corner of his mind to Parks? Would that be safe? In the end he decided there might be wisdom in giving Parks a glimpse of his mind. Parks loved to gossip; Parks would without question talk. And what Parks might say would prepare the team, in a way, for anything that might come.

"What did you expect?" he asked, feeling his way.

Parks said slowly: "I had about given up hope of expecting anything. With York out there day after day pushing you to the side—— Well, I thought that was that."

"And what do you think now?"

"I don't know—yet," Parks said cautiously.

"Neither do I—yet," Tarly said. "I've been fighting for Mountain High for three years. I might come to the conclusion that it's time I did a little fighting for myself."

That speech had been carefully made. It intimated much and promised nothing. He had not committed himself.

"In case anything starts——" Parks looked directly at him. "You ought to know where I stand."

This was Tarly's first real inkling of how the squad felt.

After that he became a sharp thorn in York's side. He questioned the methods of practice, remonstrated with maddening insistence when men were shifted about, insisted stubbornly on the soundness of his own judgment. Much valuable practice time was wasted. From the start his mind was made up that Christy Lee was to go to the first team. He had given his word that the editor was to play end; either he had to bring Christy into prominence or else admit himself beaten.

York tried hard to keep the peace. Before long, however, the goading became unbearable. When he did strike back he struck only when he and the captain were alone. Publicly he still continued to smile.

"You're continually harping on Lee, Tarly. Tell me, what did he do today that stood out?"

Tarly didn't try to meet that. He shifted to another tack. "Let's take Elliott. What did he do today that marked him as an end?"

"Many things."

"What were they?"

York struck hard. "If you knew the points of end play you wouldn't have to ask me. The fact that you do ask me shows that you are not a fit judge of whether Elliott or Lee should have the post."

Tarly flushed. As a matter of fact, the line had always been his weak spot. He had read books, made notes, and still he was never quite sure. With backfield play he was at home, but linesmen were a sort of mystery. York might be bluffing. He was not sure.

Neither was he quite sure as to how far the squad would follow him. Were they ready for a complete break? He was determined that some day he would order Christy into the first team line, but he hesitated to give the order that would bring a crisis down upon the squad. Not until he was completely sure.

Parks, smiling a sleek smile, came to his house that night. They went up to Tarly's room.

"Close the door," the back said.

Tarly objected. "Holy cow, I guess I'm safe to speak my thoughts in my own house."

"Visitors may come in and overhear me. What I have is hot, Tarly."

Tarly closed the door.

Though the door was closed Parks spoke in a lowered voice. "I heard something that might interest you. You think York is acting as a coach under full credentials?"

"Of course."

"He isn't. He came here as a physical training instructor."

"I know that. And physical instruction takes in the teams——"

"It doesn't," Parks crowed triumphantly. "His

contract doesn't say a word about coaching. He's handling the team as a voluntary job."

Tarly sat very still. "You're sure?"

"If I told you where I got that—— I can't. It was given to me in confidence. You can take my word that I'm telling you the truth."

Tarly sat there turning the situation in his mind.

"You see what this means, don't you?" Parks demanded.

Yes, Tarly saw it. He merely wanted to look at the situation from every angle and size up every possibility.

"Why," he cried happily, "York's out there with no real authority." Then Mountain High was, in theory and in fact, still his team.

After that what had been cool insolence became haughty arrogance.

York, clear-eyed, while not knowing all of the cause saw clearly what was coming. And yet he felt himself powerless to halt the insidious, creeping shadow. He would willingly have surrendered here and there on small, unimportant points. But to give an inch, reason told him, would lead to a

more insistent demand that the surrender go farther, and steadily farther. One capitulation and he
would be undone.

The bitterness of the situation lay in the fact
that, despite a murmuring undercurrent of unrest,
the team was making progress. McNichols was
learning zone strategy—the number of downs to
risk, the time to kick, when a forward pass was
dangerous and when it was the logical play either
from the standpoint of safety or unexpectedness.
Joe Macy was rounding out to the type of backfield man York had anticipated. Day by day Elliott's play at right end improved.

And a miracle had happened to the scrub. No
longer was it a flinching, indifferent skeletonized
scrub. Where Mountain had once been put to
trouble to find eleven men to face the first team,
the scrub had grown so that there was plenty of
substitute material. For the first time in its history
Mountain had a scrub touched by the magic wand
of ambition. The second string men put forth their
best efforts and fought for those places of glory on
the other side of the scrimmage line.

With so much of promise in his hands, with so much that could be lost, York felt there was nothing for him to do but go on as he had started and trust that Tarly Ball would not take it into his mad head to go running amuck.

Up to this point all the practice scrimmages had been soft. The coach had been more concerned with timing plays and seeing that each man fulfilled his assignment than with yardage results. But now these preliminary drills were over. The time had come to get down to the solid, smashing, squirming, sliding, give-and-take of man-sized football.

Overnight York became a driving, merciless demon such as Mountain High had never seen upon its football field.

No longer was each play reviewed at its completion, even sometimes stopped, to the end that men could be told wherein they had slipped or failed. Standing behind the first team he goaded and pleaded, bit it with irony, lashed it with mocking scorn. The team, stung, quickly smashed out a first down.

The fire that touched the first team consumed the scrub. Embattled, rising to unexpected heights of inspired resistance, the second string men offered a stone wall that refused to fall. Held to four yards on three downs Tarly rashly refused to admit that the long-despised scrub could hold the vaunted first team. From kick formation he tried a trick play and, in dismay, saw it smeared by a watchful end named Elliott.

The first team had lost the ball on downs.

York shifted and took his place behind the second team. "Now, scrub." His voice was the exultant call of an inspired leader. "This is your day and this is your chance. If they're no better on defense they'll be paper. Rip them to pieces."

Tarly moved behind the first team linesmen patting backs. "Steady, gang. That's onion juice."

York was talking. "What are you going to do about it, 'Varsity'? Where's this famous fighting spirit I've been hearing so much about? Got any? Let me see it. Personally, I think these scrub men are going to take you apart and make you like it. Oh! You don't think so?"

Silence from the first team. As a matter of fact the first team did not know exactly what to make of this lashing.

"Oh! So you fellows know you're going to be torn apart. All right, scrub; at them. Drive it to them. *At them!*"

The scrub play was nicely masked. Joe Macy, running with judgment behind his interference, skinned around Christy Lee's end for nine yards.

York's laugh rang loud and clear across the field. "So this is Mountain High's fighting team, is it? Where did you leave that celebrated fighting spirit, back in the locker-room? What's the matter? Have you all gone weak in the knees? Come on, scrub. Show them no mercy. This is your day to pock meat. Show them no mercy. Sock it to them again."

The scrub socked. One of the backs cleaved straight through the center, straight-armed Parks in the secondary and went on for seventeen yards. The safety man stopped him and brought him down with a vicious tackle.

York crooned. "Oh, you bully boys! Oh, you

scrub huskies! Oh, my sweet babies! Twenty-six yards in two downs. Give it to them again."

Macy got through again, this time for four yards. Again Parks was in front of the play when it came through, and again he was straight-armed and spun to the side. Macy might have gone on for another long, heart-breaking run had not an end, feinting away from the man whose assignment called for a block-out, come up on the scrub back from the side and dropped him.

"What's the matter, Parks?" York rapped out. "That's the second time you let a play run over you. Two plays in succession."

Parks stammered: "I was off balance."

"Don't you know how to get around a straight-arm?"

"But I was off balance——"

"A backfield man, right in front of the play, has no right to be off balance. Over to the scrub and see if you can learn what to do with your feet. Macy!"

"Yes, sir," Joe called.

"Over to the first team. Let me see if you know how to play a defensive game."

Macy came over to the first team on a run. He joined a group that looked at one another with startled apprehension. York was handing out judgment summary and swift. Two mistakes and you were yanked. Either you played your position as it should be played or somebody else took your place and played the part.

Usually a man coming over to the first team got a heartening call of encouragement and good-will. Macy, however, entered a zone of silence. Tarly, tight-lipped, spoke no word of greeting and the team took its cue from the captain. All except one man.

"Hot stuff, Joe," Elliott cried. "Heads up."

Tarly gave the end a black look. His mind was back to the day he had had his first talk with York. York then had pronounced Macy an undiscovered diamond. York had picked a favorite long before coming to Mountain High, and now that favorite had been grafted upon the first team. And Christy Lee had been impatiently thrust aside in favor of another.

Tarly thought he saw the whole, deep-laid plot.

This wasn't going to be either a Tarly Ball team or a Mountain High team. This was to be a York team.

The coach was urging on a delirious, excited, throbbing scrub. "Go in there, scrub, and put over a touchdown. A touchdown! You can put it over."

Tarly, savage, stood up straight and tall behind the line. The scrub coming up from the huddle to position, was arrested by his bearing. His voice came in a clear, ringing call.

"Nobody can insult us like that, fellows, and get away with it. Make him eat his words."

A panicky first team suddenly found itself welded together. A boasted fighting spirit became, all in a moment, a fighting spirit in fact. An old voice of inspiration had called to it and it was united. Nobody had ever lashed, and driven and scorned this team as York had done today. It was filled with a raging soreness and players muttered as they crouched in their places.

The scrub's first play was wrecked. A wild first team line crumpled the opposing line and three men got the runner.

"Come on, fighting team," Tarly shrilled.

"That's fighting. That's jamming something down somebody's throat."

A scrub thrust outside tackle was stopped for another loss, this time a yard. Parks, taking the ball for a third try, did not so much as get started. The scrub huddled and came back to the line, and a man dropped back to kick. And only by a squeeze did the scrub back get that kick safely away.

The safety man caught the punt and dodged and side-stepped his way back twenty yards. As players converged upon the downed ball, Tarly threw aside his helmet and, planted squarely before York, swayed lightly on his toes. A startled, ominous silence fell upon the two teams.

"Well," the captain demanded, "how do you like the taste of crow? Did we show you something? What do you think of this fighting team now?"

Somebody gasped audibly. This was open defiance and insubordination. Raw! But the coach, almost casually impassive, took the insubordination with a thin smile.

"Line up!"

Tarly continued to sway from his toes. "You

didn't mind ripping it into us before. Don't you think we have something coming to us now? You handed roses to the scrub."

The thin smile became thinner. "What does this fighting team do, ask for three cheers every time it's spurred into making a fight?"

"We'll make you eat that one, too," Tarly cried, and led the way toward where the ball lay.

York looked down at the ground. Three roads had been opened to him. He could have ignored the captain, answered him or ordered him off. To ignore the insolence would have seemed like crawling from a challenge. To have ordered the boy from the field might have brought an explosion disastrous in its consequences. Answering Tarly had been the only way. The answer had to be in the spirit of the earlier driving lash. Anything else would have been misconstrued. And yet the man knew that what he had said had probably made the situation worse.

Men walked toward the ball with Tarly, muttering again. What was York doing, coaching the first team or coaching the second? What did he think they were, a lot of poor, spineless boobs to whom he could talk as he wished? Tarly's battle cry ran like a powder-fuse through the team. Come on; make him eat it.

They were no longer fighting the scrub. They were all at once fighting their coach.

Tarly's moment, had he recognized the fact, had come.

The first team became a team gone berserk. Smash——and they were through a dynamited line; swish——and they were around Christy's end and away. In nine, uninterrupted running plays they went two-thirds the length of the field and over for a touchdown.

The second team was given the ball again, only to fall before an impregnable fortress. Runners went down in their tracks or else were carried back for bigger losses. The line became bewildered and disorganized. Parks kicked.

Tarly, with a cry of "Ho, buddies," lined up his men. They were eager, fast. Their wounds were still sore.

"What say?" the captain chanted. "Do we show York some more of the fighting team?"

"Y——e——a!" The answer ran through the line.

"He ate his words twice," Tarly called. "Let's make him eat them a third time."

Quick nods ran through the team. But two pairs of disapproving eyes—Joe Macy's eyes and Elliott's eyes——met the hot glance of the captain with an unconcealed distaste.

Oh, but they made a slaughter of the scrub that day. When the practice was over—York wisely gave them only a fifteen-minute scrimmage—a soundly whipped second team limped off toward the gym. The first team, with a first team's arrogant right, raced away for first use of the showers.

Tarly, a sweater thrown across his arm, his mouth quirked into a taunting grin, walked over to the coach. And there, in that characteristic pose of swaying lightly on the balls of his feet, he asked a question that an angry team had asked a few minutes before.

"I'd like to get a little something straightened out in my mind, Coach."

York fought down the impulse to tell the captain

there was a lot in his mind that needed straightening
out.

"Just what were you doing today, coaching the
second team or coaching us?"

York gave silent contemplation to the kick-off
spot on the forty-yards where the grass was wearing down. "Evidently you've had very little hard,
rough coaching at this school."

"That isn't what I asked you."

"It happens to be a large part of the answer,"
York answered, controlled. "Did you ever see a
clever, nagging team studiously insult an opposing
team into a blind rage."

Tarly was silent.

"Did you?"

"No. I've heard of it. It always sounded to me
like apple-sauce."

"I've seen that happen. I've seen teams so completely lose their heads that their game was hope-
lessly ruined. The man, or the team, that can't take
a riding without babying and beginning to cry can't
stand the gaff."

"This team's always been able to stand the gaff."

"You didn't stand it today. Man, what are you going to do when you face a team that goes out for goat-getting? Football isn't a silk-glove game. It's rough and it's hard; it calls for stamina, and nerve, and self-control. I want to prepare this team for everything. As for coaching the scrub—— You're not serious about that, Tarly, are you?"

"Why not? The way you talked to the first team today——"

"Do you think the teams you face are going to beg your pardon and call you 'Mister'? Did it ever occur to you that the harder I make the scrub fight you the better practice you're getting? Can't you see that there is method in what I do? If I can steel the first team to a point where it can go fighting mad and nevertheless hold its head I've made it a real team."

"*You've* made it a real team?" Tarly asked in a purring slur. "That's rather rich, isn't it? Where do I come in?"

York's temper, held in check for weeks, finally snapped. "I wouldn't call a man who babies and grandstands a team-builder."

"I made this a real team," Tarly flared, "before Mountain High ever heard of you."

York stood without moving. The crash he had dreaded had come at last. A warning voice inside him called: "Steady, steady; you may be able to sidetrack this." He did not speak.

"What about Christy Lee?" the captain demanded brusquely. "He's my choice."

The coach picked his voice carefully. "I can understand you losing your head over the practice today. You're surely not going to argue about Christy?"

"I'll tell the world I am."

"Your team went around his end six times today. He gave you four of your first downs."

"Sure he did; but that was *my* team." He stressed the "my" so strongly that there could be no misunderstanding his meaning.

A faint color showed in the coach's cheeks. "Any end who gives four downs in less than fifteen minutes would be bad against any team."

"Oh, no. That's another place where you're wrong. The team that went around him today was the team that beat everything in sight last season. Do you think any other opposing team is going to handle him in that same way?"

"I know they are."

"And it happens that I know they won't."

"Tarly," York said after a silence, "suppose you sleep on this tonight and we'll talk about it again tomorrow." He had a hope—really a slight, forlorn hope, that by tomorrow the captain would have come to sanity.

But Tarly, watching the man, knew that tomorrow the answer would be the same as it was today.

"What's the use of talking about it at all," he snapped. "You've made up your mind."

Heat crawled along his spine. Suddenly he knew that the hour for the break had come. If he were sure, if he knew exactly what he could expect from the team; not Parks and Christy Lee but all of them —— But he was not yet positive. Men might mutter, fight out on the field for him, and yet be afraid to go beyond that. He turned abruptly and walked away across the grass.

And as he went he turned the problem in his mind. He had trained Christy Lee himself and had assured the editor a place, and Christy was not to get that place. Only one person stood in the way—York. He had kept Joe Macy with the scrub, and now Joe was with the first team. The man who had overthrown him there was this same York. All his troubles could be laid to York.

The situation could not go on. If he allowed it to continue he, who had reigned undisputed and supreme, would be cheapened and belittled. The scalding practice tactics of today would become permanent; there was no knowing how many of his friends would be relegated to the scrub; the team would be driven and harassed. He would be driven and spurred along with the others. Soon every trace, every vestige of his former glory would be swept away, perhaps in time forgotten utterly. The captains before him had been nonentities. Who remembered them?

That York might be building a strong foundation on which to build Mountain High teams for the years to come did not dawn upon him. In fact, he would have been impatient of any talk of other years. He visioned only his own complete down-fall—this year.

Coming toward the gym he could hear the babel of high-pitched, excited talk. He walked into the locker-room and, as though paralyzing palsy had come upon human tongues, all talking stopped. There was an embarrassed silence.

Tarly walked to his locker. This might be his moment. He watched for signs.

Somebody picked up moleskin pants and threw them with heat and violence into a corner. That, in itself, was a violation of locker-room rules. He caught the wrath in a dozen pairs of eyes and his head came up with the old, devil-may-care snap. All right; he knew where he stood now. All they needed was a leader. He knew, as though he had been in the room, what the suddenly suppressed discussion had been about.

"What's the matter with you fellows?" he asked genially. "Are you suddenly afraid of me?"

The wrathful eyes exchanged cautious glances. "Don't you know I'm one of you? Say it. Speak out. Don't let me stop you. How do you know I don't sympathize with you and feel the same way?"

"Macy here?" a voice asked suddenly.

There was a craning of necks, a counting of noses.

"Macy's gone," came from the space in front of the lockers.

"Elliott?"

"He left five minutes ago."

But though Macy and Elliott were not there the voices ceased. Parks, still chafing from having been dropped to the scrub, proved bolder than the rest.

"We were talking about York," he said.

"Do you think you're telling me news? Do you think I'm dumb?"

Again the squad was cautiously silent.

"Don't you think I know this crowd? I ought to; I've played with you long enough. All right; out with it. What were you saying about York?"

This time the silence was profound. Tension brooded over the locker-room. Tarly reasoned that the crowd, face to face with opportunity, still feared to make the cast.

It was Parks who again voiced the mind of the group. "Is this thing going to happen every day?"

"You'll have to make it plainer than that," Tarly told them. "We want no mistakes later, with men saying they didn't mean this or that or didn't understand this or that. If there's going to be a show-down, I want a show-down that nobody will misunderstand. All cards face up on the table. What do you mean?"

"All right, then," Parks said swiftly, "if you want it straight I'll give it to you straight. Is York going to tear into us like this every day?"

"I don't think there's any question of that."

"How do you know? We want things plain, too."

"I've been talking to him. Naturally, I protested. He tells me that's his idea of how a team should be coached."

"Does he think we'll stand for it?"

Tarly swayed slightly. "I don't know. Perhaps he doesn't consider you. As for whether or not you'll stand for it, that's up to you. Will you?"

"I won't." Parks had declared himself.

A chorus of "I won'ts" ran about the room. Voices broke into relieved clamor:

"This team played good football before York ever came here."

"You never hounded us, Tarly."

"Where does he get the idea he can snap a whip and make us roll over and play dead?"

Parks spoke again. "You played me for two years. You were always satisfied or you wouldn't have kept me there. He's been shining up to Joe Macy since the first day; everybody could see that. What does he think you are, the water-boy? Where does he get off to ignore your judgment and send me to the scrub?"

Tarly's heart beat with a hard, wild rhythm. Oh, he had them now. He hadn't been forced to go out of his way to look for this chance. York had opened the door himself.

"If I do anything——" he began.

His eyes searched them out hotly, every player there, one by one. He saw that they were like sheep, waiting breathlessly for what he might decide.

"If I do anything," he went on slowly, "how

many of you are with me? Not with me tomorrow, or for a few days or even a few weeks. With me right straight through to the finish."

"I am," said Parks.

"I," said Christy Lee.

That single word, "I," became a chorus.

"Is this unanimous," Tarly asked, "or are there any dissenters? Hands up to be counted."

Every hand was raised.

"That makes it unanimous. What I will do needs a little thought. We don't want to go off half-cocked, and then find that we've slipped some place. Within a day or two——"

A shadow fell across one of the windows that faced the field.

"Here he comes," a voice whispered.

"We'll see later," Tarly said hurriedly.

They were dressing in an atmosphere of hostile silence when York walked into the room.

CHAPTER
5

Mountain High Stumbles

THE break between Tarly Ball and York, though it had threatened for weeks, came suddenly.

Up to the very moment of rupture York had hoped that the calamity could be avoided. When the string snapped, after long weeks of tension, he thought that the smash could not have come at a worse time. Tarly thought it could not have happened at a better.

For the break came on the eve of the first game of the season against Pilgrim High.

For several days an almost open spirit of insubordination had been rife in the squad. In vain the coach exhorted, pleaded and wheedled, coaxed and cajoled. Faced with failure, he fell back upon the lash. The sting of the lash failed, too. The players,

no longer responding snappily to his orders,
shrugged their shoulders under his wrath.

To this amazing extent had Tarly wrought havoc
in those few tense minutes in the gym.

He was as calloused, as indifferent as any of the
others. In the end York, completely exasperated
and with no other means in sight, sent player after
player to the sidelines. When this last step pro-
duced no change the man grew calm and lost himself in abstraction after the fashion of one who has
come at length to the end of his rope or else turns
some new plan of action in his mind.

"Tarly," he asked quietly, "are you deliberately
trying to wreck this team?"

"No," said the captain, his eyes slits, "I'm trying
to save it."

"We play Pilgrim day after tomorrow. What do
you think of that Pilgrim team?"

Tarly sniffed. "A walkaway."

"Which way?"

"For us, of course."

"What do you think the score ought to be?"

"At least forty-two to nothing—easily."

York made no comment. "Suppose you come around to my house tonight and we'll select the line-up."

"I'll see," said Tarly, noncommitally.

He did not keep the appointment. He had had no thought of keeping it. He was through with sitting in on conferences where about all he did was utter vain objections. Besides, he was reasonably certain that the man to whom he had committed himself, Christy Lee, would not be York's choice for right end and that Joe Macy would be at left-half instead of Ben Parks. Any team that York would pick could be nothing but a York team.

He had other plans. It seemed to him that the time had come to make those other plans, long delayed, a reality. Better still, he thought he saw a way to twist the break so that it would appear to the team to be of York's making and design.

The coach came to the gym next afternoon and said nothing of the broken appointment. Tarly, his nerves hard and tight to meet the expected storm, was baffled when no storm came. He watched York narrowly. The man, apparently without a worry in the world, whistled softly as he blew up a football. With the football under one arm he walked down to the door and looked out at the field. The first group of players, clumping down the room to go outside, found him in the way and moved as though to step around him.

"Just a moment," York said casually.

The group stopped.

Tarly walked forward lightly on his toes. He knew that casual tone. It usually meant something.

York had taken a paper from his pocket. The captain caught a glimpse of a list of names. His pulse jumped.

"I have here the line-up of the team that will take the field tomorrow," the coach said. He read the list slowly, pronouncing each name distinctly. Joe Macy was down to play left guard and Elliott had the place at right end.

Tarly found the eyes of Christy Lee and of Ben Parks on him. The atmosphere of the locker-room had become tense. In the silence a boy's breathing could be plainly heard. The squad, pushing closer, was held in a sort of vivid, rapt anticipation—of what it did not know.

"Not so fast." Tarly's voice had the edge of a knife. "Whose selection is that?"

The coach took his time about replying. "I invited you to my house last night. You knew that we were to pick the starting line-up. You did not come."

"I didn't see any reason to go."

"Why the sudden interest now?"

"I want to know——"

"Who picked the starting line-up should be obvious, don't you think? You weren't there. You didn't think a team selection important enough to bother about. I was the only one there. Naturally, these selections are mine."

"I thought so."

"What else could you think?"

"I don't like that list."

"You should have discussed that last night," York said quietly. "You had your chance; you deliberately refused to take it. This is the team."

"I'm captain," Tarly burst out.

"Yes; I know you're captain. There's very little chance to forget that fact. You've been announcing it to me daily."

Tarly had a conviction that the scene was not going as he had planned. Somehow York was taking the honors. Instead of declaring himself he had permitted the discussion to develop into an argument, and he had never yet been the coach's master at argumentation. He determined to declare himself now.

"This is my team," he said. "I have the right to pick the men who will play. Parks has had two years' experience with the first team. He was good enough for us before and he's good enough for us now. Christy Lee is my choice for right end. I want to play them." The declaration appeared to lack a necessary force. He changed the wording. "I'm going to play them."

A nervous cough sounded from the rear of the group. York, tranquil, gave no sign that he was annoyed. His calm glance went unhurriedly from face to face; here and there eyes wavered before that gaze and fell. Slowly and methodically he folded the list exactly down the middle, then slowly and methodically he folded the paper a second time and placed it in his pocket.

"I came here as physical director," he said. "I was not engaged as a coach. Theoretically, my work ends when I see to it that every pupil does the physical work required by the regulations laid down by the State Board of Education. If I were to make a shrewd guess I would say that you already knew that. Somebody took the trouble to have my contract looked up at the offices of the local Board of Education."

The silence grew profound.

"That was you, Parks, wasn't it?" York asked.

Parks muttered something and tried to melt into the background.

"No matter. The point is that I have no official authority. I have tried to help out. Of course, if you don't want me, that's quite another story. I can only refuse to be responsible for a team that ignores my advice."

"I imagine we'll be able to get along," Tarly said with flippant unconcern.

The break had come about far more easily than he had expected. A load left his shoulders. Tough? How had he fallen for this idea that the man was tough?

"Will you?" York asked thoughtfully.

"Leave that to us."

"Not," the man added in a musing undertone, "that I looked upon myself as indispensable. Oh, no; far from that. But you are forgetting something."

"We're going to forget a lot," Tarly told him.

"That's where you're making a serious mistake. You don't know it now; you don't see it now. Nevertheless, you're headed straight for trouble."

"Not trying to talk yourself back, are you?" Tarly asked smoothly.

York smiled. "What good would that do? You don't want me. You'll think you'll about face and go right back to where you were before I came. That's impossible. Whether you realize it or not, you've absorbed more of what I've tried to teach you than you think. You'll find yourselves complicated by two systems. The new will be clashing with the old. You'll continually find angles of play that seem to need additional development if they are to be effective; you won't know how to go about that development. You'll make a stab at traveling strange roads and you'll lose yourselves on the way. You'll be shy one of the greatest strength-giving assets a team can have."

"What's that?" a voice asked curiously.

"The spirit of working for something greater than your own ambitions—the spirit of working for the team and the school. We talked about the Pilgrim game yesterday, Tarly. What did you say the score would be?"

Tarly answered confidently. "Forty-two to nothing."

"Tell me that after the game."

"I'll wire you," Tarly mocked.

"Do," York said, unperturbed. "Send the wire collect. Well, good luck. Any time you think you need me you know where to find me."

"This team needs you now," said Joe Macy.

"That's how I feel," Elliott said.

Tarly smiled blandly. "That's to be expected

from you fellows, isn't it? All right, gang; outside. We're wasting time."

The Pilgrim game was played away from home. Somehow, nothing seemed to go right. A line that had begun to develop smoothness and coordination began to charge raggedly; a backfield that had begun to show speed and power became slow-footed and uncertain. McNichol, the quarter, developed a bad case of jitters and his handling of the ball was far from clean. At the end of a disappointing, galling half the score was 7-0. Mountain had managed to squeeze out a single touchdown.

"Isn't it about time you fellows start to play football?" Tarly snapped during the intermission. "You act as though you were never on a field before today."

"First-half nerves," Ben Parks bragged optimistically. "We've had them before. We'll get going."

The squad took it up. Yeah; the old fighting spirit! Everybody up on his toes! They went out for the second half full of a flaming spirit that had often carried them through in the past. Apparently the spirit was all they had; something, somewhere, was still lacking. They made a first down and then were halted. Tarly dropped back to kick.

McNichol's pass was so low that it almost struck the ground. Tarly lost valuable time reaching down and straightening up. A Pilgrim tackle broke through. Ben Parks, guarding Tarly's left side, found a man coming down upon him fast and, becoming rattled, dove for the Pilgrim threat. The man, neatly sidestepping that diving body, ran for Tarly and leaped. The captain had to kick hurriedly or else not kick at all; it was too late to try to run with the ball. The leather oval, spiralling up off Tarly's instep, thudded against the tackle's chest.

"Ball!" Tarly screamed in fear.

In the mad scramble a Pilgrim man recovered down on Mountain's five-yard line. And from there, in a pounding attack, Pilgrim went over in three downs.

Tarly was sick with rage and disappointment. His fury descended upon McNichol.

"Believe me, you're going to practice passing

until your back cracks. Didn't you ever handle a
ball before?" He swung upon Parks. "What was
the matter with you?"

"I missed him," Parks said sullenly.

"Missed him? You should never have gone for
him that way. Didn't York teach you never to leave
your feet?"

"Why bring up York?"

"Didn't he? Don't duck."

"I thought York was through coaching this
team," Parks jabbed.

Tarly swallowed a painful lump. "It would have
been the play that time."

Mountain High cracked wide open after that
unexpected score and was almost continually on the
defensive. Late in the fourth quarter she found her-
self inside Pilgrim's ten-yard line. All she needed
now was the punch.

The punch was not there. One play gained a
yard, the second play was thrown for a loss, a
third play died at the line of scrimmage. The angle
was bad, but Tarly tried desperately for a field
goal. The ball missed and the game was over with

a tied score. For the first time in three years Pilgrim had crossed the Mountain goal-line.

Tarly did not wire York the result.

A grim, silent team rode back on the interurban, and the captain surrendered himself to bitter thoughts. York was right. The old days were clashing with the new. It was a trap, he raged inwardly, that York had purposely dug for them. Trying to fix it so that the team couldn't get along without him. Well, they'd see about that. This was a fighting team and it had fought its way out of more than one tough situation.

Monday York came to the locker-room. Tarly, glowering, waited for a triumphant "I told you so." The man, however, asked a question that had nothing to do with Saturday's game.

"What are you going to do with the scrub, Tarly?"

"Nothing." On the instant the captain saw the chance to justify himself and also to justify the team. "That was the cause of our being beaten Saturday."

"What was?"

"Too much scrub. Last season we won our games because we were fresh when we took the field. Saturday we had gone stale. We'd left our fight back here in our own park. Let me tell you there's going to be no more of that. We'll pick a few men for substitutions and practice as we used to."

"Do you mind telling me if Joe Macy or Elliott will be among the men held as substitutes?"

"Why should I hold them?"

"I'm not asking you that. Are you going to hold them?"

"No. You ought to know what I think of them."

"Quite," York said blandly. He was silent a moment. "Do you mind if I take the scrub?"

"What for?"

"Football."

"Take them and welcome," Tarly said, "but keep out of the first team's way."

Later he was of the opinion that this decision of his had been a master-stroke. York, hovering on the edges of the team, might prove a disturbing element. But with the scrub to play with his interests and attentions would be absorbed and he would not come snooping around. They would be let alone.

After that Mountain High witnessed the spectacle of two football teams from the same school, and yet with nothing in common, practicing daily on the same field.

Down at one end, far removed from the stands, York's team reported on time and ran through stiff drills. Splitting the team in the middle the coach played one half against the other and got football practice of a sort. Students who drifted down to watch what was going on reported that apparently York was trying to build something around Joe Macy and Elliott.

Tarly guffawed. "That's a fine way to spend the season. I wish him luck."

The school, at that time, was with Tarly. The students knew the captain and were captivated by his old halo; they had not yet come to know York. The team had turned in a disappointing tie score in its first game; but then, Tarly's charge of staleness from too much scrimmage had been accepted as truth. Somebody named York's squad "the-all-dressed-ups-with-no-place-to-go." The name stuck.

At the other end of the field the first team dawdled. The iron hand of discipline had relaxed; it was human nature that the players should swing to the other extreme. Sometimes, because of the number of late arrivals, the practice did not last twenty minutes.

Common sense warned Tarly that this was going too far. For one thing a lackadaisical attitude did not look right—not with York's misfits and castoffs turning out at 3:30 each day on the dot.

Tarly tried a little discipline of his own. He poured cutting sarcasm upon late arrivals. When that failed he tried the same tactics that had won the punctuality battle for York and sent Ben Parks to the sidelines.

"I thought we were going to practice as we always had practiced," Parks grumbled.

"This team is going to practice the way I say," Tarly retorted. "It's going to get here on time."

"Copying York?" Parks sneered.

"I'm copying nobody. If you weren't dumb

you'd know we have to get some work done or not get any place."

"Who's delaying the work now?" Parks asked wickedly. "We're all here. You're holding us up with talk."

McNichol said thoughtfully: "If we're going to follow York's system what was the use of getting rid of York?"

Tarly found himself helplessly enmeshed in a web of his own making. The spirit of revolt that he had fostered and that had had its birth against the coach had now begun to develop resentment against all authority, against even him. The fighting captain found himself bewildered by the careless, slothful, contemptuous, indifferent tactics of his own fighting team.

Meanwhile, the coach went his serene way, companion, counselor and guide to every boy of the discarded scrub. If there were times when heat flamed in his eyes that heat never crept to his tongue when he met the first team squad in the locker-room. York was a patient man.

Mountain high played its second game—and

won. Barely won. The score was low, 14-13, and
again an admittedly weak rival put over a touchdown. Two touchdowns! This second game was
played at home, and almost every Mountain student saw the battle. They left the stands wondering
at the score. There hadn't been too much scrub the
past week. There had been no scrub scrimmaging
at all. What had become of the famous Mountain
punch of old? Where was the renowned fighting
spirit?

Up to this point the school had been almost
solidly behind Tarly. It was the old story—the
home crowd was with the home boy against the
interloper. Now, suddenly, sentiment split apart
and ran in three separate and distinct channels.
There were those who maintained hotly that York
was responsible for the trouble; that he had disorganized Mountain football by trying to carry
himself too high. There were those who, clearer-
eyed, began to see in Tarly's rebellion something
at odds with the eternal principles of fair play. And,
as always happens at a time of crisis, there were the
weak, shivery, hesitant souls who waited to see

what would eventually happen before declaring themselves for or against the principles of Tarly Ball.

By Monday all shades of the school gossip had crept to the captain's ears. It was a new and disquieting experience to find even so much as a small minority of the school condemning him. It brought him up with a turn. It cleared his vision and focused his eyes on facts that he could no longer ignore.

The team was playing poorer football than it had played this time a year ago—poorer football than at any time since Tarly had become captain. Instead of improving with the Pilgrim game it had, if anything, gone back. The spirit of cohesive team-play had grown perceptibly thinner; they seemed to be eleven men, each playing solely for himself. Timing, that all-important element in attack, had become monstrous and weird. Runners ran into their own interference; interference was not around at the moment it was needed.

Last week Tarly had laid the blame at the door of too much scrimmaging, too much scrub. Yet, since the Pilgrim game, the team had done little else but run through signals. He could not claim that a stale team had made a sorry mess of the second game. It was a team that was not geared as a team should be geared.

Tarly had lost his fight for punctuality. While waiting impatiently for his men to gather he lurked in the doorway of the locker-room and watched York's scrub. Down at the far end of the enclosed field they seemed like pigmies going through a slow-motion drill. And yet, though the practice was made vague by distance, the conviction grew upon him that the scrub was serious—far more serious than his own team. He saw, too, that it seemed to have developed a disconcerting smoothness, and he had a cold, gripping memory of a time when his own team had had that same smoothness. He swung toward the room.

"Who are we waiting for?" he asked.

"Parks," Christy Lee answered.

Parks, Tarly thought in growing resentment, was always late. And yet, from the day York had sent him off, York had had no further trouble with the halfback on that score.

Parks strolled in nonchalantly. "Some of the campus buzzards are beginning to give us the hooks," he announced.

"What kept you?" Tarly shot at him.

"Why—nothing."

"Don't you know we're supposed to begin practice at 3:30?"

"Sure. We're always supposed to begin at 3:30."

"Why can't you get here on time? You've held up the whole squad fifteen minutes."

Parks looked surprised. "Why pick on me? Anyway, I'm getting tired of being the goat. Am I the only man who ever held up this squad?

"You held it up today. You hold it up oftener than anybody else. There's been too much loafing. That's what's wrong with this team—too many of you fellows thinking you can do as you please."

"I thought it was too much scrub practice," Parks said with a leer.

Tarly choked. "I'm getting the idea you don't know how to think. Hereafter, I want all of you here on time. Do you understand that? I'm speaking particularly to you, Parks."

"Say," the halfback demanded angrily, "what's the idea? Who do you think you are?"

"I'm captain of this team."

"Oh, no. You think you're somebody else. You think you're York. I don't know how the rest feel, but for me, so long as we're through with that bird, let's stay through with him. We don't want any second-fiddle Yorks."

Again Tarly found himself helpless and impotent. He could drop Parks, but who did he have to put in Ben's place? Joe Macy? But Macy, rejected, was at the other end of the field with York's scrubs; and he would have cut out his tongue before he would have admitted to York that he was wrong and have asked for a player he had cast aside. He gruffly ordered the team to the field.

Parks strolled out smiling.

That day's practice became a haunting nightmare. Men loafed, and sulked, and missed the signals. Parks had lighted a spark and, twice that afternoon, heated quarrels broke out among the linesmen. Students thronged the sidelines and listened in.

And all the while, at the far end of Mountain Field, a toiling scrub, with York following in its wake and correcting mistakes, worked without dissension or hitch.

Next day a chalked scrawl was on the bulletin-board in the main hallway of the school:

SCRAPS! SCRAPS! SCRAPS!

ANYBODY VS. ANYBODY

MOUNTAIN HIGH FIELD

ADMISSION FREE

Tarly's face went white.

Mountain squeezed out a victory in its third game by a score of 20-14. Victory was snatched from the depression of another miserable tie in the last two minutes of play. Tarly, dressing after the game, still trembled from the spectre of a defeat so narrowly averted. There had been sorry lapses, inexcusable and stupid. One of the other team's touchdowns had been an outright gift.

The Mountain locker-room, accustomed to merriment after a victory, today was acid with strife.

Bitter quarreling, always on the surface lately, again broke out among the players and they began to blame each other for the day's disasters. Once Parks had fumbled and charged that a poor pass from McNichol had caused the error. Tarly, jumping in between the two angry men, had difficulty in preventing a fist fight.

"Perhaps," Christy Lee said timidly, "they were a whole lot stronger than we expected them to be."

"They weren't strong," Tarly said bluntly; "we were weak." Perhaps he could burn them into a realization that they would have to stop this sapping internal warfare and begin to play together. "We were rotten."

"So what?" McNichol snorted. "Who was the particularly rotten apple in Mountain's barrel? I think that every one of us knows the answer to that."

Tarly found himself wishing he had not stopped the fight. McNichol was the smaller and would probably have taken a beating.

"Listen!" he snarled. "I'm the captain of this

team. Any time there's criticism to make I'll be the one to make it."

McNichol brushed that aside. "Where did they make a whole slew of their gains? Wasn't it around Christy's right end? Didn't anybody ever tell him an end is not supposed to let himself be outflanked? Can't he understand English? The interference played him for a sucker."

Tarly flushed.

"Anyway, didn't York always claim he wouldn't be able to break up interference? Isn't that the reason York didn't want him on the first team?"

Christy stood there in helpless distress. But his distress was no worse than the captain's.

"Another word out of you——" Tarly began thickly.

"Oh, yeah?" McNichol laughed. "A lot I care. Maybe York could use a quarter down at the other end."

Parks took a new tack. "I think I'm beginning to see what's the matter with this team."

Tarly's pulse throbbed. He had fought for Parks,

but of late the halfback had begun to rasp his nerves.

"Suppose you tell us what we need," he challenged.

"Work."

"Oh! Just like that, eh? Just work."

"We've gone rusty. We've let ourselves get soft. We were insane to fall for that stuff about not scrimmaging with the scrub. You can't sharpen a blade without a hone."

Tarly Ball was badly stung. "I didn't hear you talking that way two weeks ago."

"Nobody talked that way then."

"In fact, Parks, you were the player most anxious to bring on a break with York. You told me the team would be with me. You brought me the information about York's contract. Now that things are growing tough you're becoming wormy. You're beginning to crawl. Why didn't you do some of this talking when York asked me could he have the scrub?"

Parks shrugged. "You were the captain. I thought you knew what you were talking about."

"I didn't know any too much when I talked up for you. In every game we've played you've messed up plays. In every game you've tried to blame somebody else. I fought York for you, but I'd give five dollars right now if I had Joe Macy."

"Why don't you ask York for him?" Parks invited.

Once more Tarly was helpless and impotent. He wouldn't ask York and Parks knew it. The captain wished for the second time that he had let the fight go on. Perhaps both of them would have taken a good licking.

"Have you noticed," McNichol asked, "how York's got these scrub fellows going along——"

Now the fighting captain was recklessly, heedlessly ready to fight. Fighting eyes froze the quarterback. The flame of those eyes went from man to man, daring, challenging.

"Does anybody else want to take a chance on a few more criticisms?" the captain asked furiously.

Nobody answered.

He went home with the quarterback's words hammering and clanging in his mind.

So York had the scrub going smoothly! He didn't have his team—not as he had had it a year ago or a year before that. A year ago he could have given an order and have known that that would be the end of it. A year ago his team was a fighting team that fought opposing teams. Now they quarreled and bickered among themselves. Eleven men pulling eleven different ways! They fought each other and they fought him. Today he had so far forgotten his own sense of values, his own position, as to quarrel with them. He had been ready, for one wild moment, to use his fists. He could not imagine any of them, least of all Parks or McNichol, standing up and talking back to York.

That night he tried in vain to concentrate on a lesson in physics. He shifted to history with no better results. He couldn't control his thoughts and hold them to a set channel. York's prediction seemed to shout at him out of the thin air:

"You think you'll go back to where you were. You can't. The new will be clashing with the old."

The new and the old had clashed. But that had been at the beginning. Now the team itself was clashing. It had never quarreled in the old days; it had never broken out into dispute in the new days under York. This was a new development. He could blame nobody but himself. The internal strife of the team had broken out under his leadership. His and nobody else's.

He pushed the books aside. Study was useless. He sat, lost in thoughts of what might have been.

Fear came to him and ran cold, clammy fingers along his spine. Fear of the future as that future would undoubtedly affect the Mountain team; fear of that future as it would certainly affect Tarly Ball. Tarly Ball, the fighting captain!

The weak-sister part of the season was over. The teams they would encounter from now on would be much stronger. No need for him to ask himself what chance Mountain High would have playing in its present form. He knew. And when the defeats began to pile up, and the team lost heart and went to pieces entirely, what would become of a fighting captain's reputation?

Fright whispered to him to save himself and to go to the coach and humbly ask for help.

And then abruptly his courage rallied—— Well, not so much his courage as his pride. His pride revolted and called halt.

He would not confess defeat. He would rally the disorganized team. He would still fly his imperial flag of leadership. He would fight this fight through and find a way to win out in the end.

But his lips, and his mouth and his throat were dry with an aching dryness.

6

Tarly Surrenders

NEVER, in the years of his undisputed leadership, did Tarly Ball work as he worked now.

The result of the third game, the fury of passion let loose in the locker-room after the game, awakened him from a dream. Events that followed close upon the game showed him that he stood on the edge of a precipice and had begun to slide. When you slid off a precipice that was the end.

He could feel the end coming. For suddenly there was no more singing of "The Fighting Captain of a Fighting Team." Suddenly there was only a fringe of students alongside the sideline to watch the practice of the first team. Suddenly the crowd was far down at the end of the field where York worked with a thoroughly willing squad that was all dressed up and had no place to go.

Tarly tried everything. He tried again to get the squad to report on time and succeeded, not because of his ability to persuade but because the desertion of the student body had stung. He walked them through plays over and over, increased the tempo, finally ran the plays at speed. They clicked. His spirit soared.

"Again," he cried. "The whole string."

Parks tripped over a trailing foot on the first play. "Get out of my lane and stay where you belong," he snarled at Christy. Christy, usually the mildest of the players, snarled back. The quarrels and contentions flared up like a flame. And the rest of that string of plays stalled and fell flat.

"Heads up," Tarly told himself. "Tomorrow you'll have them where you want them. You almost had them there today."

But the tomorrows began to click along through the week, and there were no consistent gains. After each outburst of quarreling, listlessness and indifference increased.

The day came when Tarly closed both the gym

door and the locker-room door, and turned a key in each lock.

"What's that for?" Parks asked. There was a continual insolence in the halfback's manner akin to the insolence that Tarly had once given the coach.

"You'll learn," the captain said.

"Oh, I see. Deep, inside stuff. Going to break it to us gradually?"

Tarly held his temper. "There's nothing like taking precautions when you want to make sure nobody walks in with good ears and then goes running around with a tale. You've noticed, of course, where the crowd has drifted?"

"What's the matter with them?" McNichol asked sourly. "We're winning, aren't we?"

"Fair weather friends," a voice hooted.

"Fine Mountain men," somebody else taunted.

"They're flocking to the team," Tarly stabbed, "that doesn't put on a free-for-all every afternoon. How many games do you think we're going to win, from now on, unless we pull ourselves together?"

"Professor Ball," Parks chirped, "will now give his bad, bad boys a slap on the wrist."

"Shut up and listen to him, you trouble-making ape," Christy Lee shouted across the room.

"You call me an ape——" Parks plowed forward.

Tarly caught him by the shoulders. The same old story! He had to fight harder at that moment to hold his temper than he had ever fought to win a game. There was a bench to the side. Without appearing to do so he exerted his strength and pushed Parks toward it. The halfback, in spite of his struggles, sat down hard and looked at Tarly with a new respect.

"Parks has the wrong idea," Tarly said. "This isn't a joke." A good thought, this turning the moment into harmless humor. "It's serious. McNichol says we've won. There's a lot of honor in that. We've played three teams and we haven't played enough good football to score a touchdown on any first-class outfit. We have two victories. Both of them were scratch victories. Both were scored against teams that should have been set-ups. Anybody want to boast about those two victories?"

His vehemence held the squad to silence.

"The school isn't dumb. They know we're doing a bum job. They don't know that York's outfit would be any better; but they do know that something's gone wrong with us and they trail away from us in the hope that they may find something going right with York. If we were winning as we should be winning they wouldn't so much as give York a second glance."

"To heck with them!" McNichol cried. "We can get along without them. Who do they think they are?"

So that was to be the reaction! Discouragement almost made Tarly weak. You talked to them, you tried to make them see what was so apparent, and all you got was "To heck with them!"

"Why shouldn't they follow York?" the captain cried passionately. "What do they see? They see York's squad out there on the minute and working long and late."

"We've been coming on time," Parks observed.

"Since when? These last few days? York's squad has always been on the dot. They see this team start after York's and see York's men still at it when we quit. They see this team stroll out, drift aimlessly and get no place. There's no question about what we must do. We must put on our own show and take York's play away from him."

"If I might ask you," McNichol said with mocking politeness, "what is to be the first act of this play?"

"Get out here on the field before York."

"What does that mean?"

"It means to report fifteen minutes earlier."

"Why not report early in the morning," the quarterback asked, "and not bother with classes at all? That would have York licked. His squad does go to class."

"Of course," Parks sneered, "the school will be so dumb it won't know we're aping York."

"I don't care what the school thinks or knows," Tarly shouted. "They think enough hard things about us now. At least we'll be making a stab at trying to play football."

McNichol raised an eyebrow. "Trying?"

"You heard me."

"Better go easy, Mac," Parks advised blandly. "Papa's on the warpath. Papa spank."

The temper that Tarly had held in check by a supreme effort of will flared and sizzled once more. They'd make it a joke, would they? Clown around while he was trying—trying——

"All right," he cried, "if you think this is funny I'll show you that it isn't. Practice hereafter is at 3:15. The man who isn't here at 3:15 can turn in his uniform."

"Do you think you can get away with anything as high and wide as that?" Parks demanded.

"Try me," Tarly challenged hotly. "As sure as there's a tomorrow I'll drop the man who reports late if I have to stick in his place some freshman who's never had a football in his hands."

They knew that he meant it.

Afterwards, looking back on the scene, Tarly felt regretful and bleak. Things had come to a fine pass when players and captain wrangled like alley cats.

However, next day the team reported on time. Parks, with studied ease, walked into the locker-room exactly at 3:15. He dressed with great de-liberation.

"We're waiting for you," Tarly called.

Parks glanced at the clock. "You said 3:15."

"You're holding us up now."

Parks, unhurried, laced up his moleskins. "Why didn't you tell us we were to be time-clocked get-ting into uniform?"

Once more the spark of rebellion had been struck. The practice ran along in sullen undertones. Mutterings rolled like thunder through the line and fumbles marred the work of the backfield. Then, as had happened at other practice sessions, the team began to miss its signals. Misplays were followed by altercations that interested the handful of stu-dents that still followed the team.

And at the other end of the field the scrub went about attending to the work York had given it.

"I wonder," Parks said aloud, "if you haven't made a mess of all this, Tarly?"

"Why me?"

"Well, you're the captain. You led us into this."

"Did any of you object to being led? Didn't

some of you urge me to make the break? I'm not trying to get from under; I'll stand or fall on what I've done. Anyway, if we have made a mess of things, it's too late now."

Instantly he saw the pit into which he had plunged himself and was furious that the admission had been wrung from him.

"I see," Parks said meaningly. "Too late."

"I mean it's too late to expect any help from York," Tarly cried. "I mean this is our party and it's up to us. We have the power. We're the same team we were last year and the year before. We haven't begun to use our power, that's all."

They didn't use it in the fourth game, either, and were lucky to get away with another tie score. The sun in the eyes of a man all set to take a high, loping pass, interception of that pass by Christy Lee—this had given Mountain a tie.

Tarly, fighting as he always fought, today a burning brand among faint embers, could not win the game alone. Christy's interception of the pass gave him a momentary gleam of self-satisfaction. He had taught the editor how to make those catches. But his own pet play, a sharp slant off the opposing left tackle, had been smeared time and again because Christy failed to take out the defensive half. And three times the rival team, sweeping down upon the right end, bewildered Christy with interferers and outflanked him for long, damaging gains.

Today, instead of quarreling, the players trudged to the locker-room and went under the showers in a silent depression that met the drab apathy of the stands. Suddenly Tarly wished they would break into the old frenzy of bitter wrangling. At least, when they wrangled they were alive, they had movement, they had fire. This way they were dead and ready to be buried.

The scrub could not get its usual long practice the day of an at-home game. But even on game day York managed to get in something. With the field cleared and the crowd gone he took three men out; and now those in the locker-room heard the dull thud as the three men kicked.

McNichol began suddenly: "I wonder if——" He checked the words as abruptly as he had begun.

"So do I," said Parks.

Tarly swallowed. The muscles of his throat were tight and swallowing was hard. Here and there players watched the halfback and the quarterback and he knew that the same thought was in many minds. He knew what the thought was. He could ignore it, or he could force it out into the open and fight it. He decided to fight.

"What do you wonder, Mac?"

McNichol cleared his throat and hesitated. Well able to do his share once a battle started he had always flinched from firing the first shot of a war.

"Oh, tell him," Parks cried impatiently. "What's the sense of beating about the bush. Mac's wondering whether, if we went to York—— Well, there it is."

Yes; there it was. The drip from the showers seemed unnecessarily loud in the unnatural silence.

"Is that quitting talk?" Tarly asked in a strained voice he did not recognize as his own.

"What do you think it is?" McNichol asked coolly.

"With Mountain playing Southside and Valley its next two games? Do you two mean to tell me you're confessing that you're licked?"

"Aren't we?" Parks demanded.

The captain's red hair seemed to become an unruly, riotous torch. "I'm not."

Nobody spoke. That, in itself, was mute testimony of how thoroughly he stood alone.

"If any of the rest of you fellows are wilting—— Oh, don't be cold fish. Don't hide. Step out. Open up and declare yourselves. Whoever's wilting, whoever hasn't the guts to go on, step right out and say so now."

The group stirred restlessly. Slowly, reluctantly, Christy Lee came forward a scant step.

"You!" Tarly cried.

"I—I'm afraid I'm no good, Tarly."

Whatever the captain might have expected, this was the last man he would have picked to come forward. The room blurred and he swayed a little on his feet.

"They're making their gains through me," Christy said with an effort. "If it were only one

game—— But it's every game. I'm afraid I'm a drag
on the whole team."

"He's afraid he's a drag," McNichol mocked.

Parks' voice had a nasty edge. "I could have told
him that three weeks ago."

Tarly boiled. "Did you see him pick that pass out
of the air in today's game?"

Parks snapped: "It's about time he did something."

"If he hadn't picked that one today's game
would have been lost."

"If he could play his position we'd have walked
away with every game we've played so far."

"Who are you to criticise anybody, Parks? If
I had Joe Macy you'd have been out of the line-up
a week ago."

"And if I knew as much last September and could
have my vote back perhaps you wouldn't be captain."

Tarly shook. "Who let Pilgrim through to block
a kick? Who lost us the Pilgrim game? We should
have won it. Who's made a hash of defending the
kicker all season?"

"Is it my fault," Parks shouted, "if it takes you a month of Sundays to get a kick away?"

Tarly found ice along his spine. Once more he was in a shamelessly rowdy brawl with the players. Good grief, what were they coming to?

"Listen, Parks." He was pleading.

"I won't listen to anything."

"You've got to listen. We've all lost our heads and we're all saying things we don't mean. We're all sore and mad because we're not clicking. That's all right with me. You know it's all right. I wouldn't give a dime a dozen for players who can take a licking and think it's funny. You talk of sending for York. What can York give us? A fighting spirit? We had that before he ever came here. Instead of fighting the teams on our schedule we're fighting each other. Sure, we have lots of fight. We always had lots of fight. We're not using it the right way. I don't mean to fight Parks; he doesn't mean to fight me. We're both on the ragged edge." He held out his hand. "Right, Parks?"

The eyes of the left half blinked. "Right," he said, husky, and gripped the captain's hand.

"Want to count me in on that?" McNichol asked.

The captain's other hand went out to the quarter. The recollection became a love feast, and the silent depression of the shattered team turned into a gay channel. Somebody banged a cleated shoe against the metal of a locker door, and a voice cried: "Yeah! We're on our way." Christy Lee led the singing of "The Fighting Captain of a Fighting Team."

On the way home Tarly's footsteps pounded out a refrain on the concrete pavements. "Go to York; go to York; go to York." That's what the demoralized players wanted—York. A coach to come and try his hand at saving them. Well, he had been lucky to talk them out of it today; but he saw, with the clarity of desperation, that he would not be able to talk them out of it again. He had to produce results and the time was short. With only two games left—Southside and then the enemy of all enemies, Valley—whatever he accomplished had to be done with amazing speed. For unless he led the team to victory against Southside next Saturday——

And then there was Christy Lee!

Christy had struck him a staggering blow. Coming from the friend for whom he had risked so much and dared so much, the friend whom he had gone out of his way to personally coach, the protege whom he had called fit, the blow still left him numb. It showed him the depth of the doubt that had seeped into the team; it showed him, too, the depth of the inroads that had been made in Mountain's celebrated fighting spirit. If Christy Lee began to doubt and to question, what could he expect of the others?

Regret burned him. He had been wrong about Christy. Oh, how he had been wrong! He had made a rash promise, and had been ready to risk wreck and ruin to keep that promise. Christy wasn't a good end. Christy would never be a good end. York had called the trick—Christy could not handle interference. York, he knew with a feeling of despair, had been right about Parks, too. But what could he do? If he took Christy out, who did he have for his place? And if he took Christy out it would be an open admission that he had been grossly wrong. In the present temper of the team he couldn't make such an admission—not after Ben Parks' violent attack on Christy today. To make a change now would be a confession of weakness. It would give color to the thought that he had ceased to lead his men and merely followed where they pointed out the way.

He wondered if he really did lead, or if his leadership had degenerated into an empty, meaningless mockery.

His footsteps took up the refrain: "Go to York, go to York, go to York." His eyes, even though they recognized the line that separated him from complete failure, grew stubborn and hard. His pride called out of the past a colorful picture of sustaining grandeur—the intoxication of going along an aisle and up to the auditorium platform to dominate a cheering student body; the victory dinners given by the Merchants' Association after two seasons; the golden glorious prestige that came to one who was the fighting captain of a fighting team that did not fight in vain.

Let him beat Southside and all would be forgotten. Let him ride his team over Valley and all Mountain would bow down at his shrine in humble homage.

"No," he said. "I won't go to York. I'll fight it out. I won't be made cheap."

Christy Lee came to his house that night. The editor was nervous and apprehensive.

"You're not sore at me, Tarly?"

The captain was silent a moment. "Why did you throw me down today? Didn't I have enough on my hands with Parks?"

"I didn't mean to throw you down. You asked—— I am a drag on the team."

"You're not," Tarly cried fiercely. So long as he had to use Christy he would do all in his power to strengthen the editor's faith in himself. "You've been an unfortunate victim of bad breaks. Perhaps the tide has turned. The breaks came your way toward the end today. You saved the game."

The visitor drew a deep breath.

"Christy, I'm going to ask a frank question and I want a frank answer. Do you think you owe me anything?"

"I owe you everything," Christy said without hesitation. "You did all you could for me."

"Then do something for me," Tarly said slowly, "and the books will be all-square."

"What do you want me to do?"

"For the rest of this week I want you to play in the practice with your whole heart. I want you to keep talking it up, to keep the pep going. The old tabasco! No matter how tired you become I want you to fight off any temptation to let down. Will you do that for me, Christy?"

"I wish I could do more," the editor said fervently.

Tarly went to sleep that night with the thought that at least two of Mountain's men would try to make what was left of this week's practice what practice should be. He and Christy. Three short days in which to prepare for Southside. Three days in which to climb to the sunlit heights of his old kingdom of glory, or see that kingdom, tarnished and shattered, pass out of his hands.

He worked, during the days that were left with a tireless zeal, a desperate persistence. When the team gathered for the next afternoon's practice he met the players in the locker-room with a swaggering display of masqueraded confidence, a fixed and twisted grin.

"Hi!" he called.

"Hi!" shouted Christy.

"Everybody on his toes. We're going places. Grab your ticket and climb on the train."

"Grab your ticket!" Christy shrilled.

The players took on an air of expectation, an aura of confidence that reflected the captain's. They charged out upon the field like men who had been galvanized and remade.

That day they tried. Something magnetic in Tarly Ball at his best enveloped and warmed them and lifted them far above themselves. The plays swept along with power and zest, the line was fast and purposeful, the backfield was almost perfect in its timing. And once Tarly got off a long, soaring punt that fell to the ground thirty-seven yards away.

"Hi!" Christy Lee yelped. "What will Southside do against that kind of kicking?"

"We'll have them back in their own territory all afternoon," Parks exulted.

Tarly felt a fresh flow of power that strengthened him and gave him new life. That's how a fighting team went on to glory. The right type of captain inspired the team; the team in turn climbed to rare peaks and lifted up the captain.

"Fellows," he cried happily in the locker-room, "we're clicking at last. We're on our way."

The team, still in a fervid glow, began to chant a song of doom for the mighty Southside:

Another little job for the undertaker,
Another little job for the casket-maker——

It was, Tarly told himself, like old times.

Rain fell next afternoon in a sodden, steady drizzle. The gloom of the gray, dank outdoors crept into the locker-room, and a team that had played for one afternoon beyond itself began to slough off and lose its zest. Reaction set in—a reaction of lethargy that was made even more deadly by the dreariness of all outdoors. Tarly, swinging into the locker-room with eager steps, was conscious at once of the sagging change. Good grief, were they going to go dead again?

"Practice today?" Parks asked.

Tarly affected an air of surprise. "Of course. Why not? What does rain mean to a football team?"

"Oh, I don't know. You get all gummed up, and it's easy to twist around in the mud and sprain an ankle."

Tarly hid the stab of pain and cracked the half-back playfully across the shoulders.

"When was Mountain ever afraid of a wetting? Suppose it rains Saturday? Got to play the game just the same. Everybody put on strong ankle bandages. This will be fun."

The fun must have hidden itself away under the damp, dripping stands. After yesterday the practice was a tragedy. The men were slow and spiritless. The wet ball was hard to handle and fumbles predominated. Time and again Tarly dried the ball with a towel, but that helped only for a moment. Men slipped and had trouble with their footing, and twice Parks sprawled into his interference. He began to jaw at the interferers and his interferers jawed back. Tarly, afraid that too much damage might be done, cut the practice short and ran the soaked players back to the gym. He would have outlawed practice today and have concentrated on a blackboard talk, only time was so short. So agonizingly short!

"York's still out there putting his men through formation," called a voice from one of the windows.

"He's welcome to all he wants of it," Tarly said bravely. "I thought to give you a taste of skidding in case we have to play on a muddy field next Saturday."

All the way home he talked fervently to himself, bringing a battle-cry from the depths of a stout heart that could still fight. "We must win the Southside game; we must win the Southside game." No going to York now but "We must win the Southside game." Over and over again as though by calling insistently for victory he could bring victory to rest upon Mountain's banners.

Next day the field was almost dry. The team, following a flaming leader, reached for the power and the drive it had commanded forty-eight hours before. Christy Lee talked and talked until his throat was hoarse; Parks panted, and struggled, and gave all that he had to give.

And yet today they were ragged and raw.

What made the collapse worse was that today the team was really and sincerely trying. There had not been a single outbreak of quarreling. Sweat dried on Tarly and he began to shiver. The old machine was there, the same Mountain machine of last year and the year before that, but now the various parts had developed burrs and rough spots and could no longer work smoothly.

In the end, with an unconsciously weary motion of his hand, the captain called the practice to a halt. And the players, instead of trotting off to the locker-room, stood looking down the field to where the work of York's earnest scrub was followed by a gallery of more than two hundred students.

"We must win the Southside game." Tarly's

soul no longer called a battle-cry; now it breathed
a prayer. The prayer kept him up in the locker-
room where men donned street clothes in a
thoughtful silence. And then, suddenly, even his
strong heart faltered. The prayer changed to a
hope. "If—if we can win from Southside."

He dared not allow himself to think of what
might happen to him and to Mountain in the event
of defeat.

Friday night the land soaked under a steady
downpour of rain. At ten o'clock Saturday morning the sky broke, a wind came out of the west, the
sun came forth. Tarly, on a tour of inspection,
found the field a sea of mud. Hope crept out of the
dark shadows and held forth a slim possibility. In
mud as deep and as slippery as this anything could
happen. Slow men might become mud-larks, fast
men cripples. A team, intrinsically inferior to its
opponent, might slip and slide through to a victory.

The team, in the locker-room, had the appearance of a team afraid of what the next few hours
might bring.

"Aren't you fellows glad you had your fifteen

minutes in the rain?" Tarly demanded. "You know the feel of mud."

"What does that get us?" Parks asked. "They've had their experience squirting around in mud, too."

"Oh, no," said Tarly. "I invested fifty cents this morning and put through a telephone call to South-side." That was a lie. "They haven't had rain in a week."

"Who did you telephone to?" McNichol asked suspiciously. "Southside High? They probably told you that so as to throw you off."

"Do you think I'm a ninny?" Tarly grinned. "I telephoned the office of the Southside *Sentinel.* I've got it straight. No rain for at least a week."

Tarly could see the team rouse itself and begin to hope. He could almost tell, by their faces, the exact moment they began to dream.

Out on that field of mud the dream died. It died quickly. For three minutes after the kickoff South-side had spattered its way across the goal-line for a touchdown.

That day, face to face with certain defeat, Tarly Ball really earned his reputation as a fighting cap-

tain. But the stands were blind to the drama per-
formed under its eyes. All the stands saw was a
team that had once been great going down to
slaughter. They did not guess that one flaming soul
fought heroically to the end against the inevitable.

The final score was 21-7. Tarly had plowed
through Southside for Mountain's lone touchdown
and then successfully kicked for the point after
touchdown.

Back in the gym the team hung about and did
not undress. Tarly called: "You fellows had better
get under the showers before you chill," but they
paid no heed. Parks, almost absent-mindedly, kept
tapping his shoes against a bench and knocking
splotches of drying mud from between the cleats.
York, with a few of his men, had taken possession
of the churned, trampled field. Tarly, at a window,
ripped off his jersey and stared out forlornly at
the mocking goal-posts.

"Shot to pieces," Parks said at last.

Tarly caught his breath.

"I'll say we're shot," McNichol said savagely.
"We played out there today; we gave our best.

Well, what's the answer? We're not good enough any more. Parks is right—shot to pieces."

Parks kept tapping his shoes against the bench and looking down at the drabbled cleats. "I'm not saying anybody's to blame more than anybody else. I guess we all went hay-wire. We didn't know when we were well off. We all wanted a change. We certainly got it."

"I'll say we did," came from McNichol. "Last year we gave Southside the works. The sports writers said we were on our way to be one of the greatest prep school teams of the State. I wonder what they'll say in tomorrow's newspapers?"

"What can they say?" Parks grunted. "Twenty-one to 7. That says all that's necessary."

Tarly turned from the window. There was still one Mountain trench untaken, still one tomorrow that was theirs.

"Listen!" he cried hoarsely.

Parks ceased tapping the shoes.

"I know how badly things look. But perhaps they're not as bad as they seem. That game today wasn't a fair test."

"I wish I could believe it," said McNichol.

"You've got to believe it. You can't judge by a game in the mud. The ground slides out from under you; no team can play its true game. A man headed straight for a yawning hole slips; a slippery ball that is passed perfectly true is fumbled. A mud game is a luck game. Why, you can see how we're coming along. They didn't get around Christy once today."

McNichol shook his head. "I wish I could believe you, Tarly," he said again. "But a mud field is too slow a field for wide end runs. They used a few plays off the end to throw variety into their attack. That's the answer. They didn't expect those plays to gain. It wasn't the day for nice work around the ends."

Tarly closed his eyes for a moment. "All right; let's admit we were rotten today. Other teams have gone through a rotten season and then found themselves at the last moment. Notre Dame did it against Army a couple of years ago. If we—"

Parks dropped the shoes, and sighed, and stood up. "It's no go, Tarly."

"Why not? You saw how we came back this week in practice. There's always a chance."

"Not with this team. We're shot. S-h-o-t! There's no use in your trying any longer to kid us and certainly you'll be a fool if you keep on trying to kid yourself."

Tarly wet his lips. "What do you want?"

But Parks, always bold and ruthless with words, came to a moment when he could not speak the truth outright. When he did speak his voice was strangely gentle with regret.

"I'm sorry, Tarly. I'd keep away from this if there was a possible chance. But if we had York back——"

That was all—just an unfinished sentence.

Slowly, amid a silence almost breathless, Tarly walked to a bench and sat down. Presently one of his hands made a slight gesture and fell to his side.

"Get him," he said. Only those nearest him heard his voice. "He's out there with some of the scrub kickers."

7

York Resumes Command

IT SEEMED to Tarly Ball that long, leaden hours passed while they waited for the coach to appear.

The showers in the locker-room had always dripped. Today they dripped with a spatter more dismal than his own thoughts. This, then, was the end of the road that was to lead to a fresher sparkle to his crown.

He thought of one of the paintings that hung in the main corridor of the school, "Napoleon at Waterloo." He had been an emperor, but his empire was gone.

Parks, paddling softly in his bare feet, carried his shoes over to a locker. Christy Lee looked at the captain once with misery in his eyes and then stared down steadily at the floor.

Tarly wondered if they could hear the hard, fast, painful throbbing of his heart.

Outside footsteps sucked at the soft ground. A shadow fell across a window. The door opened and York strode in.

An electric current ran through the room. Tarly, wide-eyed, gave the man a slow, fearful scrutiny. He was honest enough with himself, human enough, to hope York would not gloat. One moment of smirking "I-told-you-so" and whatever hope Mountain held in York would be completely undone. Whatever happened now, it seemed to the boy, was in the hands of the coach.

There was nothing of triumph in York's manner. He stood by the door as casually as though it were a daily event for the squad to send out for him.

Tarly was glad of that. The man's attitude made everything easier. And yet, when it came time for him to speak, the words stuck in his throat and would not come at once. His pride writhed in its dying agony.

"They—they want you back," he said with a visible effort.

"How about you?" York asked quietly.

Tarly saw what lay behind the apparently simple question. The man was taking no chance of future denials of intent and of present misunderstandings.

Everything had to be in black and white. The captain could understand that. He had taken the same attitude when Parks began to hint that the squad was ready for rebellion.

He nodded slowly. "Yes. I want you back."

"Why?"

Nobody answered. Why tell him? He had been in the stands today and, if he had an ounce of brains in his head, he ought to know.

And apparently York did know. He let the question die.

"I wonder," he said thoughtfully, "if you've given any thought at all to what the after effect would have been had your action this fall been successful?"

Again nobody spoke. Tarly wondered if York's casualness was a mask and if the man really intended to rub it in.

"You would have established, probably for many years to come, a principle of mutiny."

"Oh, come now," Parks broke in irritably. "We sent for you because we've learned we've made a mistake. We want to be friends. Mutiny is putting it too strongly."

"It can't be put strong enough," York said quietly. "You would have riddled the theory that a team owes certain loyalties to captain, to coach and to school. You would have written the logic that a team need answer to nobody but itself. And like all mutinies it would not have stopped at its original goal. It would have gone on."

"I still say you're putting it too strongly," Parks broke in.

"Am I? Let's see. I have not tried to shadow this team nor have I sought for information. Yet no man in close touch with a football situation at a school can help hearing the news of what's going on. Originally, you mutinied against me. Your next step was to mutiny against Tarly. Had you ever fought his authority as captain before? Why did you fight it since the Pilgrim game? Because the principle of mutiny had been established. The next step would have been mutiny one against another. The formation of cliques, and after that cliques would begin to gang up on this man and that man. When you reached that point you would have come to anarchy."

Parks was silent.

"I'm no fool," York went on. "When the summons came I knew what it meant. I didn't come in here to lecture. But certain things must be said now. You questioned my statement as to the effects of mutiny. You see what it has already meant in your own team. What of the future? I don't mean today or tomorrow; I'm speaking of the far future. Take a look at that future. Next year most of this team will graduate. You will depart; but your influence will remain. And that influence, like some chronic, wasting sickness, would remain to rob Mountain High of strength and inspiration."

Feet shifted nervously. Tarly was conscious of a slow, burning flame creeping up his neck.

"Have you ever seen men leave a game sobbing because they could give no more? I have. Have you ever heard college men sing their hymn on the night before Commencement and seen the tears in their eyes? I have. That's when men love their school or their college. This love fills them with a clean spirit of self-sacrifice. It is one of the richest experiences that can come into a young man's life. And what was your response to this great emotion? What did you do? You failed to recognize it. You tried to strangle it. You tried your best to poison it here at Mountain."

Behind Tarly somebody caught his breath with a choking sound. The captain thought of Christy Lee.

"I must use plain words," York said. "I don't like to use them. I dislike even so much as the appearance of mocking at men who are down. I am not mocking. I must make you see the truth. None of you was thinking of the school or of what you owed to the school. You were thinking of yourselves. And now you're afraid the school will turn on you and call you to account, and charge you with failure. You're afraid to face the consequences of the piracy on which you so boastfully started.

The handwriting is already on the wall. It was on the wall weeks ago when the students deserted you and began to follow the scrub. Why? Don't you know? Can't you see why boys and girls deserted the first team and came over to watch a team that had no place to go?"

"I can see it," Parks said bitterly. "After winning for years we had begun to take the short end. The school is like everybody else—it has no use for a loser."

"Did the school expect the scrub to be a winner? Of what?"

Parks had no answer to that.

"Oh, no; the school didn't desert you because you were losing. The school deserted you because it recognized in the scrub the spirit that you should have had—but didn't have. I'd told my boys they were the men Mountain would have to rely on next year and the year after. That didn't mean anything to Macy and Elliott. They graduate in June; they won't be here next year. But Macy and Elliott have the spirit; the entire scrub has the spirit; and the students recognize that spirit unconsciously and flock to it as though it were a beacon. No school can be great without it." He looked at them long and steadily. "No player can be worth his salt without it."

There was a painful silence. Christy Lee sat down and held his head in his hands. The flaming burn had left the back of Tarly's neck and he was clammy and cold. Outside the scrub boys could be heard patiently kicking the ball—practicing for next year and the year after that.

"If I come back," York said suddenly, "I want one fact understood—that I come back on my own terms. I'm not trying to force anything down your throat. You don't have to accept me. If you don't want me, if you think I'm too severe, I can go back to my own boys."

"My own boys!" Nothing that York could have said could have better marked the distinction.

Parks looked quickly at Tarly.

"What are those terms?" the captain asked.

"I am to be the boss. The sole boss. I say that because indications are that two heads would be worse than none. We tried dual authority before.

I am to give orders and make selections as I see fit. I am to answer to nobody and there is to be absolutely no interference. Do you agree to that?"

One by one heads nodded. Some nodded quickly; some nodded slowly. One head—Parks' head—did not nod at all.

"Mind, I am to consult no one."

Tarly swallowed a lump in his throat.

"As for the Valley game——"

The silence that had been painful now became profound. The thud of a kicked ball sounded with startling clearness as though the punter were here in the room.

"I have no confidence in you fellows," York announced abruptly. "Why should I? You have no confidence in yourselves. If you had a single shred of confidence left in all the squad you would not have sent for me."

Still that profound silence.

"You're doing exactly what I told you you'd do—you're trying to play two different brands of football at once. You're bewildered. I want a team that plays but one style, knows only one style, thinks of only one style of play. I want a team that knows that one style thoroughly and plays that one style consistently from kick-off to final down. I know of only one team at Mountain High that comes up to these specifications."

A sudden, startled stir, a shocked gasp of incredulity, ran swiftly through the squad.

"You mean——" McNichol began in a low voice.

"I mean that next Saturday I'll throw in the scrub against Valley. Not because they're my boys, but because it's the only team that really represents this school and because it happens to be the only team that Mountain has in shape to play any kind of football at all against anybody."

"That's too much," Parks broke out angrily.

"Why?"

"That means that you'll junk this entire team."

"Well? What of it? Are we here in the interest of the school or of this team?"

"But you'll be throwing aside a lot of good men. I've played my position for two years——"

"I've watched your play all season and I've never thought you were a particularly good man. You're a pants-slapper. When you carry the ball you slow up and flinch an instant before you're hit by the tackler. When you're the man to make the tackle you flinch——"

"Do you mean that I'm afraid?" the halfback cried out.

"No. What you do is done from habit. I could have cured you of that. Now there's no time. I could have cured you, too, of your weakness in defending the man who is to punt. Once more, however, there's no time. I never called myself a miracle man. You can't cure bad football habits in a day."

Parks' face had whitened. For him he recognized a sentence—he would not be in the Valley game.

"While we're on this subject," York said, "let me offer a suggestion. Some of you will go to college; you don't want to carry along football habits that will doom you in the college game. If you wish it, I'll come out here with any of you, after the season ends Saturday, and coach you against your weaknesses. In time those can be cured."

But Parks could think only of his banishment. He swung toward the captain.

"Look here, Tarly——"

"You wanted him back," Tarly said.

"I know, but——" The left-half faced the coach. "We sent for you to come back and coach *us*."

"When I walked into this room," the coach said coldly, "you told me only that you wanted me back. You did not say I was to coach this team. Had you made that proposition I would have refused it. Some of you would scarcely be worth bothering with."

Parks leaped forward in front of the captain. "Do you hear that? He's saying you don't know how to pick men. Look here, Tarly——"

Tarly Ball shook his head. They had taken York back on his own terms and they had understood what they were doing. The thing was done. Besides, his team had passed out of the picture. He knew that for truth.

"You mean you're going to let him get away with this?" Parks demanded, aghast. His voice changed to lashing, bitter scorn. "So you're the stuffed shirt we always called the fighting captain."

Tarly's face was the face of a stricken man.

Without a word he got up from the bench and walked past York out of the room. Scrub players were still kicking a ball around. Not scrub players now but first-string men! There was a place in back of the stands where relief pitchers warmed up when it looked as though Mountain might have to make a battery change. He paced this strip of secluded dirt until the last player was gone.

Then, coming back to the deserted, forlorn locker-room, he dressed—alone.

One sentence the coach had used stuck in his mind and would not be shaken loose. No player lacking in school spirit is worth his salt! He thought that out in frowning contemplation and, lost in the occupation of thought, forgot temporarily the isolation in which he now found himself. For the present he had lost sight of the fact that he was a captain without men to command, a general without an army, the ruler of an empire whose realm had been laid waste.

In the dawn of another day he awoke and began to wonder what the school would think of this change in its teams.

He did not have to wonder long.

The school found something of the strongly dramatic, something of glorious hazard, in the prospect of an unknown, untried scrub stepping in and making a last-minute stand to stave off the threat of defeat. That afternoon, in a cheering, wildly enthusiastic mob, the school paraded to the field to give encouragement to its raw, unseasoned warriors. For the first time that season there was uproar and excitement comparable only to the din, frenzy and clamor of one of the season's big games.

Tarly, watching from the sidelines, thought that the school had never turned out like this for his team—not even in the good old days of last year and the year before. They had had a strong following, of course, but not the whole school. Had he carried the thought a bit farther he would have seen that the team had set up an aloof aristocracy all its own and had never really been closely knit with the school itself. But the team now practicing on the field was the school.

He watched the scrub that day as he had not watched it since the day of the split. It wasn't the

same scrub he had given York. In the end he was
forced to admit to himself that these men showed a
singleness of purpose that had been foreign to his
team. They had a rhythm that his team had lacked.
The fact seemed incredible. How could any scrub
team be better than a first team?

York met him at the end of the practice. "What
do you think of them, Tarly?"

The captain hedged. "I've seen them only once.
It's hard to get a line from one look."

"That's true; but how do they look to you on
the surface?"

"They seem to be an improvement over the gang
that were working for me," Tarly admitted grudg-
ingly.

The coach's eyes softened. "Study them. You
may find weak spots I have missed. No coach can
see it all. A break in the pattern escapes him. There
may be a man or two on the first team who would
fit in better."

Tarly knew that no man from a team that had
tried to play two kinds of football could fit in better than a man who had played only one kind. York,

evidently, was trying to make him feel that he would have a voice though his would be truly a minor voice. He was grateful for the man's consideration. Parks caught him in the locker-room and tried to draw him aside. He shook off the halfback's hand.

"Don't be silly, Tarly. There's no sense in you and me keeping up this fight. We both want the same thing."

"What thing?"

"Well, call it revenge. That's as good a word as any. York has kicked both of us out. Oh, we can hang around in uniform, but do you think that means anything? Saturday we can sit back and see his little pets get murdered. It won't be our funeral."

"Suppose the scrub isn't murdered?" Tarly asked.

"The scrub? Are you going nuts? Wake up and be yourself. Do you think any scrub has enough class to go out there and hold up against Valley?"

Tarly gave him a long look. "You don't want to see them beaten, do you?"

"If you don't want to see them massacred," Parks said coldly, "you're dumb."

"I guess I'm dumb, then."

"Look here! What happens if they're swamped? I mean a darned good swamping? Before the sun goes down Saturday the school will be doing a wailing act and weeping about how it should have kept its first team. We'll go right back in the saddle like circus riders. It won't do us any good this year; the season will be over. Anyway, we graduate in June. But there's a next September. We'll be the heroes who might have done the job if we had not been tripped."

"We tripped ourselves," the captain pointed out honestly. "We invited York back."

"Don't be such a ninny," Parks snapped impatiently. "Won't the school forget that? They'll elect a new captain right after the game. Who's going to elect him, our crowd or York's crowd? If we're back in the saddle we can pretty well dictate who next year's captain will be. It won't be one of us—we'll be gone—but we can say who the captain will be. And York will find himself out in the cold."

But a streak in Tarly recoiled. He would have none of the plot.

At home a copy of that day's *Argus* lay on the porch floor. He opened the newspaper to the sports page. A picture of York and a headline leaped out at him:

TARLY BALL DETHRONED
IN MOUNTAIN HIGH SHAKEUP

The captain's eyes grew hard. York's picture— and always the picture that went with a Mountain football story had been his. So his downfall was to be cried aloud through the countryside. Always he would be known as the captain who had not been strong enough to hold his authority.

A new thought struck him. He went to the telephone and called Christy Lee's house.

"Was that your story in the *Argus?*"

"No."

"How did they know what had happened? You cover the school don't you?"

"I had to turn in the story that—that York was back."

"Oh!"

"Listen, Tarly," the editor of the school paper pleaded, "I didn't write it the way it was published. I made it short—I merely said York had been invited back to prepare the team for the Valley game. Somebody must have smelled the trouble and sent a reporter out on it. I had to turn in the news. I couldn't throw the paper down."

"I suppose not," Tarly said after a moment. "Isn't there a reporter on the paper who knew York out west?"

"Yes—I told you that."

"I see it now," said Tarly and hung up. Had York given the reporter the twist that featured his dethronement? Remembering the man in the locker-room he couldn't believe this. But his lips were hard again.

"Perhaps," he said harshly, "a good, sound beating is just about what York's scrub needs."

Next day the coach gave him the signals. "I may need you and one or two others, Tarly."

He took the signals home and studied them. He had a quick mind; and besides, they were based on a system he already knew. By bed-time he had mastered their mysteries. And the next day York called him into the signal drill.

"Trying to use me to speed them up," he thought. Well, he wasn't falling for anything soft like that. If York was a builder, let him do his own building. The first play swept out and had to drag him along.

"Not so good," was York's comment. "Let's walk through it this time."

The captain flushed. A noisy student body would notice the team brought down to a walk and would make a fairly accurate guess as to what that meant. They'd be saying that Tarly Ball was too slow. He walked through the play once, then York called for faster action. His eyes snapped. As the ball left the center's hands he was in motion, timing himself beautifully and accurately.

"Better!" York cried. "Faster now."

The pace snapped. Tarly had always prided himself that he was fast, but now he had to go at his best to hold his own. Sweat soaked through his uniform; small, salty rivulets ran down into his mouth. At the end of the session his chest heaved and he panted.

"What do you think of them?" York asked him for the second time within two days.

Tarly said: "They can step."

"Is that all you see?"

"What else is there to see?"

"But the spirit, man," York cried. "Working for weeks with never a game in sight, never a moment of promised glory. Working because some day in a far, dim future they would stand for the school. What do you think of that?"

"Why, I haven't thought much about it," Tarly said, hesitant. "It's all mighty fine, I guess."

Abruptly the coach left him and walked toward the gym.

There was another headline in that night's *Argus:*

YORK'S MEN COUNT ON
SPIRIT TO BEAT VALLEY

York's men! York's spirit! Tarly Ball, apparently, was already gone from the scene and forgotten.

The captain's eyes flamed. A player without school spirit wasn't worth his salt. Why didn't York stand forth in the open and speak the truth? Why didn't he say a player without York spirit? That's what he meant.

"I hope," Tarly cried in a sudden passion, "they smash your little goody-goody team to a pulp."

The Valley game was played on Mountain Field. Superbly confident of victory, the visiting students came swarming into the stands as though the game was a mere formality—over already in all except going through the motions and the crown of victory already theirs. There was a note of joyous hysteria in their uproar, and the Mountain cheers were feeble in comparison. When Mountain sang—today she did not sing "The Fighting Captain of a Fighting Team"—the chorus of her united voices scarcely penetrated to the Mountain locker-room. The students that had followed York's scrub hoped; that was all. And hope never has the wild ring of certainty.

Valley was certain. Valley was noisy. Valley was sure.

Tarly's lips twitched with an acid smile.

He watched York, and he watched those who once had been the scrub. Elliott lay back on a bench staring at the ceiling. Joe Macy's lips moved soundlessly. The thought finally came to Tarly— an almost incredulous thought—that Joe was praying.

The acid faded out of the captain's smile.

York had gone among them examining padding and bandages. The clock on the wall announced that the time to go out on the field had come. York faced the players soberly.

"Men," he said, "I'm not going to say much. There's very little that can be said. Everything that could be said has already been said by the way you've worked. What you do today, you do for Mountain High. Not for me. Forget me——I don't count. A year from now I may be coaching somewhere else. But wherever I go, the school will remain. Every yard of ground you defend is Mountain ground. Every yard you gain is a yard of homeland recovered. For there is only one Mountain and she is ours.

"Valley expects to win. That's natural. She knows Mountain has had a disappointing season, but there are several things she does not know. She does not know you. She's over-confident, and an over-confident team is easily upset. She takes into account everything but Mountain's unshakable, unbroken spirit. Don't be afraid to kick. Joe Macy's foot can be trusted. When you use your running plays use them with no uncertainty; smash into her with everything you have. Take chances. If you can surprise her and score in the first few minutes you'll throw her into a consternation from which she may never recover. Play the game. Play the game as you know how to play it. You are Mountain's hope. Tonight you must be her pride and her boast."

Tarly heard every word of that throbbing talk.

As he listened he watched the team with a growing wonder, a dawning comprehension. In their faces, upturned to the coach, he read eagerness, and rapture and exaltation; and reading all this, he all at once felt small.

He trotted out with the team, down the long field to a roar of welcoming sound. And all the while his senses reeled and groped as though he had seen a vision.

He forgot that this was the first time in three years that Mountain had taken the field without Tarly Ball in the starting line-up. He forgot that today he sat as an unnoticed substitute, forgot all save those rapt, eager faces in the gym. York had a name for the miracle, spirit, and he had sneered. He wasn't sneering now.

By and by somebody nudged him and he sighed. He was on the bench, a blanket about his shoulders; the team was on the field spread out in a long, thin line for the kick-off. A whistle shrilled, the line trotted forward, the crowd broke into a pandemonium of cheering. The ball arched lazily into the air from Joe Macy's foot, the ends raced away toward where the ball was settling and Valley men converged in front of the receiver and tried to ward them off.

The game was on.

Parks, his voice throbbing with excitement, spoke in Tarly's ear. "Here's where they get it."

Tarly did not hear. His eyes were on the play. His fingers clutched his knees. An inarticulate cry came from his suddenly awakened soul:

"Come on, Mountain! O Mountain, come on!"

8

Tarly Finds the Road

VALLEY caught the ball on her ten-yard line, fanned in an arc up to the fifteen and then went down. Elliott, feinting past two men, made the tackle.

The scrimmage lines formed and the stands came to their feet. The roar of the crowd was deafening. Tarly saw the Valley quarter, cool and undisturbed by the uproar, look around to see that his backs were placed properly. He made a motion and one of the backs moved a little to the left. Suddenly he bent down behind the center to take the pass.

The lines broke, bulged and swayed. For a moment it looked as though somebody was coming through. There was a tangled confusion of piled and sprawled bodies and then the shrill call of a whistle. The sprawled bodies slowly found their feet and the buried ball came into view.

"How much?" Tarly demanded.

The man on his left cried out joyously. "About a yard—maybe a yard and a half."

Again the lines formed and broke. This time the play was a drive off tackle. A man, hunched over, shot out toward the end and for an instant the stands thought he had the ball. There was another period of confusion, another period of untangling scrambled bodies.

Excited comment broke out along the Mountain bench:

"No gain."

"Yah! Yah, is this man's team playing football?"

"Did you see Joe Macy dive in there and back up the line on that play?"

"We're holding them! Are we holding them?"

"I'll say we are."

"Boy, just watch us holding them."

Valley, after a long huddle, came back to formation and a player dropped back ten yards to kick. Of course, this might be a fake from which they

would launch a running play. Grandstand quarter-
backs argued hotly. What, a running play on third
down from the fifteen-yards? That would be sui-
cide.

The ball was passed back from center to the
kicker. The Valley backs spread out for a possible
forward pass. But the kicker's foot swung and the
ball spun high into the air.

And suddenly the field rocked and shook with
a Mountain cheer. Mountain had met the first assault and had checked it. The cheer, rising on a wild
note, spoke of the incredulous dawn of a hope vast
and all-embracing.

Mountain had the ball now in the center of the
field, and Tarly wormed to the edge of the bench.
The hands that clutched and clawed at his knees
had begun to tremble. Amid the uproar he could
not hear the signal, but he noted the position of the
Mountain backs. It might be Joe Macy storming
forward to take the ball in a slide off tackle or it
might be a criss-cross.

The play was the criss-cross calling for speed,
perfect timing and perfect handling of the ball.

Elliott, Mountain's right end and his tackle, teaming together, had opened a hole wide enough for an ox. Macy, the left-half, taking the ball from Coons, the right-half as they passed each other, went through that hole for six yards.

The bench went wild.

"Hi, boy! Wasn't that a darb?"

"Too fast for them. We're the speed boys."

"Fooled them completely. They were looking for the play at the other end."

"Did you see Macy stop that one?"

"Are we good? Are we?"

Parks spoke again in Tarly's ear. The captain could not hear. He leaned closer.

"What's that?"

Parks repeated. "This can't last. It's a flash in the pan. Valley hasn't thrown off her early-game nerves."

Tarly yanked his blanket free, stood up deliberately and walked along the bench to the other end. Parks' eyes followed him. He sat down without a backward glance.

On the next play Joe Macy, doubled over so that

he was all back and shoulders, smashed into the center of the Valley line and made two yards.

"Who says Valley's so hot?" a voice demanded.

Another voice shouted: "We'll cool her down."

Tarly shook his head. He was a football man and he knew that the defense had stiffened. He saw Coons take the ball, this time for a swing around the end, and make a scant yard and a half. It was fourth down and only eighteen inches to go.

The bench was silent.

Tarly sweat. He wished that York had Mc-Nichol out there now. McNichol was a tough man to handle, with a tongue almost as nasty as Parks' tongue, but he was a football veteran and could be counted on to use his head. An untried quarterback like Grant, lured by the distance to be gained, might try a running play. What, only half a yard? But there was a large chance, a very large chance, what with the way Valley was now meeting the charge, of not making that fraction of a yard; and the difference between a successful kick and losing the ball on downs would be almost forty yards. Forty long, slow, laborious yards.

Tarly scarcely breathed as the team came out of the huddle. The players stepped up to the line smartly. And then, abruptly, his lungs were full of the sweet fall air. Macy had dropped back. It was to be a kick.

The ball, riding well, tumbled deep and far into Valley territory. Valley had possession on her ten-yards.

"We've got them with their backs to the wall again," one of the substitutes squeaked.

"We gained five yards on that exchange."

"Where's this man-eater of a Valley team that everybody's been talking about?"

Tarly hugged the blanket. Oh, but York had taught these scrub boys some football. Wise football. Football that held its sanity and didn't allow itself to be led astray by willful promises. Let the kids alone—they'd play the game.

A voice whispered hoarsely: "That Valley gang means business this time. Look at them."

The side of the Mountain line went down as though ripped apart by a gale. Macy, in the secondary, got away from an interferer and ran the play toward the sideline. There he spilled the runner after a seventeen-yard gain.

Tarly tried to swallow and couldn't.

Another play, starting out wide as though it intended to sweep around the end, suddenly veered and struck between tackle and guard for nine yards. The score-board announced second down and one yard to go.

The bench wasn't silent now. It was frozen into a stark, deathly stillness.

Tarly sat in agony. If this kept up——

The ball was snapped. Elliott, waiting only to make sure that no attempt would be made to outflank him, moved in like a flash behind the Valley line. Tarly, with a cry, sprang to his feet. He saw the end, running with amazing speed, overtake the play from the rear and spill it for a seven-yard loss.

And now it was third down and eight to go.

The captain sat down. What he had just seen had removed the last scales from his eyes. He had fought for Christy Lee, broken with York partly because of him. He stared at the ground. Why, it might take all of two years before Christy would have anything like the speed and the skill of Elliott.

A roar of voices, and he snapped up his head. Valley had been forced to punt, and Mountain was in possession of the ball down on her own thirty.

The din from the stands grew. Yah! Mountain had halted the Valley machine again. A cheer rolled out for Elliott.

But Tarly, frowning, kept clutching at his blanket with stiff fingers. Mountain had been in midfield and now she was on her own thirty. Twenty yards lost. The stands weren't thinking of that. But Tarly knew that a machine that could smash out seventeen-yard and nine-yard gains could not be halted forever.

The lines moved together and took form. There was a momentary lull in the clamor and the voices of the boys selling soda pop could be heard clearly. Grant's voice came across the field thin and distance-softened:

"Eighteen, 24, 9, 64."

Tarly was on his feet once more.

The Mountain quarter had called the signal for

a forward pass. Of course, York had told the team to gamble, but this looked like a gamble with the stakes too heavy. The team had been instructed to do the unexpected, to take desperate chances, but this was too desperate. They were too deep in their own territory. If the pass were intercepted it would mean almost a certain touchdown for Valley. A score so early in the struggle might decide the game.

And then, all at once the ice was gone from his veins. His blood flamed with wild, fighting fire. Oh, but this was glorious nerve. Nerve and courage and cool assurance, and a clear understanding of all the risk involved.

Joe Macy had dropped back into kick formation. Tarly was unconscious that his lips moved and that he talked to himself. If Valley would only make a hard try to break through and block that expected punt. Such a play would leave her that much more open.

The ball was snapped.

Tarly's hot eyes saw the Valley line smash forward and fight to get through to block the kick. To the stands there was nothing to be seen but a maze of struggling bodies. To the captain's practiced observation the whole maneuver moved with military precision. He saw Mountain check just long enough. Then a Mountain end was going down the field and Coons was only a few yards behind. Joe Macy had begun to run backwards with the ball.

A warning shriek came from a player on the Valley team. "Forward pass!"

Tarly shouted and his voice was lost in the wilder shrieking of the raving stands. Nobody heard his voice: "Not too fast, Joe. Take your time. Nobody's noticing Elliott; nobody's near him. They're all going the other way."

No; nobody apparently was paying any attention to Elliott. With Valley men boiling down upon Coons and the left end, Elliott moved out aimlessly, apparently without speed or intention, a lone, forgotten figure. Forgotten until Macy, throwing a soft, flat pass, heaved the ball toward him.

Then a volcano exploded.

Instantly a loafing, lone player was galvanized into action. He ran back, paused, timed the ball and leaped. The brown oval was in his hands, hugged against his chest. The safety man came in upon him with desperate speed. He angled for the sideline and, without warning, crossed his feet, brought himself around and was off on a new track. The safety man, unable to check his charge, plunged ahead and was out of the play.

And then it became a heart-gripping race.

In feinting and foxing the safety man, Elliott had had to swing back toward midfield, toward the Valley men who had shadowed Coons and the decoy end and they were now plowing toward him. He jockeyed again, gained a little ground, lost what he had gained. One from the rear, one ahead and slightly to the side, they caught him between them at last. He fell and rolled, and carried the two tackles with him.

Tarly wasn't interested in the roll. Tarly had marked where Elliott's body had first struck the ground. The captain babbled:

"Down on their eight. Put it over, Mountain. Oh, what a honey of a play. What a melon! Put it over; put it over. Come on, Mountain. Over, over, over."

The cheer leaders had lost control and the Mountain stands were delirious. The band crashed into music and the music was lost. A corner of the stands began to sing. The song spread, jubilant and full of ecstasy:

Another little job for the undertaker,
Another little job for the casket-maker——

Tarly had ceased to babble. A broad back squirmed and writhed beside him on the bench. He pounded that back happily.

"Everybody," he called. "Everybody in on this. Everybody, now. Low, and hard, and lift them. Over."

The player undergoing the pounding seemed unaware of his punishment. He smiled blissfully. Later he might wonder why his shoulders were strangely sore, but now the pounding did not matter.

York had predicted that an unexpected setback

would throw the Valley team into consternation. His prediction proved true. Everything that York had said since the season opened, the captain thought, had come to pass.

For the captain could see that Valley was unsettled. Dazed, almost. Her captain called for time out, hoping to steady his startled, demoralized team.

The Mountain band had won control. The music stopped, and cheer leaders took control. The stands barked out a short, sharp cheer:

> Rah, rah, rah,
> Rah, rah, rah,
> Rah, rah, rah,
> Elliott

The time-out period expired. Valley came up to the line slowly. Tarly could see Valley men shifting as though still unsteady and doubtful.

Mountain struck like a whip. One blast, and Coons was through the tackle hole on his side of the line for six yards.

A Valley boy started to rise, sank back and lay prone upon the ground.

Tarly said to the player next to him on the bench: "Hooey! That fellow's not hurt. They want more time." A man in a white sweater ran out to the prostrate player with a water-bucket. A knot of Valley men gathered about the scene. Presently the player sat up. Supported by two teammates he limped about the field. Tarly muttered: "A good act. I hope Grant don't fall into a trap and think that lad is groggy."

The score-board gave the game as second down and goal to go. And only two, short skimped yards to goal!

The Mountain stands were in turmoil and Tarly found he could not sit down. Teams had been held on the two-yard line, on the one-yard line. Wasn't it Harvard who had once been held only inches from a score? But the new rules, allowing an incompleted pass over the line without the penalty of loss of the ball, would force the defending Valley to open up.

The teams faced each other across the No-Man's

Land that held the ball. Elliott drifted out wide. The Valley end had to follow him or risk a man in the clear to take a pass. That left a yawning, open spot.

Joe Macy, slashing at the open hole between tackle and end, went down under a swarm of bodies. Was the ball over or had it fallen short? Nobody knew.

And then Tarly saw the referee, his arms above his head. The boy ripped off his blanket and waved it madly.

Mountain had a touchdown.

A band blared and Mountain sang again. The air came with ragged rhythm for nobody paid attention to the cheer leaders whose arms rose and fell to the beat of the band. But Tarly, catching the volume of the crowd's joy, stood stiff and straight. Something in the heart-eager sound spoke to him as no school song had ever spoken before, not even the song that had been his, "The Fighting Captain of a Fighting Team." His sight grew blurred and he did not see the successful try for point after touchdown.

Numerals went up on the score-board.

Mountain 7; Opponents 0.

Once more Mountain kicked off. But now Valley, the worst over, had recovered her poise. Her attack upon the line was savage. She was suddenly a lion balked of her prey, but back upon the scent. Back to make the kill.

Rip—and she was through the guard-tackle hole. Smash—and she had dynamited her way straight through the center with a power play. Three times, while Mountain implored and begged her warriors to "Get that ball, get that ball," she made a first down.

And then, with the shaking stands asking if this was to be an irresistible parade the length of the field, Elliott again smelled out the play, broke through, and brought down the runner for another disastrous loss. Valley was forced to kick.

Tarly breathed through white, parted lips. Facts were facts, and you couldn't get away from them. His football brain told him what his heart did not want to believe. Valley had the better, the stronger team. York could fashion no more surprise attacks. There could be no more miracles.

And yet there was a miracle.

An outclassed Mountain team refused to admit that it was outclassed. It slipped back and held, retreated and rallied, fought and heroically advanced. Three times there seemed to be no question but that now Valley must score; and three times, when the moment came, Mountain met the shock of battering play and held it to no gain. Three times, when on the verge of collapse, she called upon some unseen power that Tarly could not understand, and three times that power saved her.

When the half ended the bold, white numerals upon the scoreboard stood unchanged.

Mountain, recognizing the miracle, sang in choking, throbbing emotion:

> Mountain, forever fair,
>   Thy name in glory shrined;
> Mountain to do or dare——

Again Tarly's sight was misty with a stinging blur. The team passed into the gym first; he followed with the substitutes. And the school hymn, pouring from thousands of fervent souls, was the last sound he heard as he passed through the door.

He sat off to one side, alone, while York worked over the team, examining bruises and adjusting bandages. Parks, passing him, gave him a sneering smile.

"Playing along with York, aren't you?"

"I couldn't play along with a better man," said Tarly.

"Huh! That's hot. Taking it on the chin and liking it. Holding out your mug for more. What a heck of a fighting captain you turned out to be."

"I wonder if you know what you've turned out to be?"

"I'm not yellow, anyway."

Tarly let the stab pass. His mind was concerned with thoughts of much greater moment. His own team, not only of this year but of other years, had had no such reserve of endurance. It had not been able to rise above itself and hold hard when all

seemed lost. It had never been able to call forth
from some mysterious reservoir a strength alto-
gether beyond understanding, a strength far, far
beyond belief.

As he watched the team being rubbed and rested,
he was acutely aware of the same rapt exaltation,
the same unconquerable force, augmented rather
than weakened by the strain, the fatigue and the
anxiety of the battle. And all at once he understood.

These men of the scrub were crusaders. They
gave without stint and gloried in the giving. They
played, not for themselves alone or for a selfish
crown, but for something infinitely greater. The
team's heart and soul were wholly wrapped in an
ideal that invigorated it and endowed it super-
humanly.

At that moment Tarly Ball, who had thirsted for
the rich trappings of lordship and authority, knew
that lordship and authority were meagre indeed.
Crumbs! What counted most was the school. The
team, as it went out to start the second half, gave
him the impression of men bravely following a star

that hovered above a land he had never before discovered.

The stands greeted the team with the familiar
hymn:

> Mountain, forever fair,
>   Thy name in glory shrined;
> Mountain, to do or dare——

Tarly paused at the bench and, forgetful of where
he was and of the crowd, stood with his face turned
toward the sky. York, happening to glance for a
moment toward the bench, saw him. The coach
spoke something softly under his breath.

The song ended. The teams ran through signals
for a moment and then spread out for the kick-off.

Somebody said: "Where's Parks?"

Another voice answered: "He was in the locker-
room. I saw him there."

"Didn't he come out?"

"Search me. He ought to be here."

Tarly, searching along the bench, did not see the
halfback. Parks, evidently, had decided to dis-
appear rather than risk the galling sight of a possible

Mountain triumph. It was, the captain thought, just as well. The man who wasn't with Mountain today in this game was against Mountain.

As long as the school endures, Mountain will tell of that second half—of how a straining, reeling, gasping, weary, outclassed team met the shock of assault and stemmed it for a while, only to break and fall at last before the fury of Valley's attack. Valley was on the twenty-three, the eighteen, the ten, the five. The trembling stands cried their imploring prayer aloud:

"Hold them, Mountain! Hold them, Mountain! Hold them, Mountain!"

But Mountain could not hold. A halfback, running behind a web of interference, rode over Elliott for a touchdown.

The end dropped to the earth and sat there, his knees drawn up, his head buried in his arms.

There was a lump in Tarly's throat. Wasn't it York who had told them of men who came sobbing from a game?

"Poor kid," he muttered. "You certainly gave

everything you had." What a game Elliott had
played. What a game! What a Mountain man!

"I—I guess they've got us now," a voice quavered
from far down the bench.

Tarly flamed. "Who said that?"

McNichol looked at him with mute, stricken
eyes.

"Mountain's never licked," the captain cried
fiercely.

His eyes burned. He continued to stare at Elliott.
And when the end arose and walked to his place
for the kick-off, a warm, pulsing glow started at
the base of his skull and ran down through his tin-
gling body until it reached his toes.

No; Mountain was not yet whipped. Oh, no—
not yet.

The stands, expecting collapse and the end, were
amazed at still another source of strength. Where,
the bewildered sports writers asked in the press
box, had Mountain found it?

Tarly knew. With every shock of play his body
strained and ached as though he were out there help-
ing. A voice announced fearfully that there were

only four minutes left to play. He shuddered as though he had been struck.

"Only four minutes?" He glanced for verification at the score-board.

The truth was there. Only four minutes! And as he watched a quarter of a minute slipped away.

A shadow fell across his knees. His lips were drawn back—a fighting man's lips—and he did not see the shadow.

"Tarly!"

He did not hear.

"Tarly!" York's hand was on his shoulder.

He gave a start and turned his head.

"Warm up," said the coach.

The blanket was gone from his shoulders and he trotted with high steps alongside the sideline.

A shrill treble pierced the din of the stands and reached his ears. "Put it over for Mountain, Tarly."

He recognized that voice—Christy Lee's. So the editor had found it, too.

Three minutes left.

Three minutes and a frenzied Valley team, frustrated in its reach for victory, laboring to change the mute testimony of a score-board that read:

Mountain 7; Opponents 7

The seconds flew. Valley had the ball. Had she been in the lead she would probably have stalled and tried to hold to the ball, but now there was no reason for stalling. A frenzied smash at the Mountain line brought seven yards. He lined up fast. Smash into Mountain while Mountain was reeling.

Her eagerness undid her. Gambling that she could outspeed and out-maneuver an exhausted, staggering opponent, she threw a long, wild forward. Elliott had spotted the play. He was out of the line running back, back——The ball weaved and wobbled through the air. Lunging sideways his hands found the pigskin, juggled fearfully for a moment, held. Spinning about on his heels he came racing up the field.

Tarly had ceased to warm up. His mouth was open but no sound passed his lips.

Elliott had to come through mingled Valley and

Mountain men. No interference had time to form for him. Coons, coming to his feet, tried to get into the play and was struck by a shoulder. He went down.

Elliott ran on as he had started—alone. The stands had gone mad. Far, far up the field from which the white stripes had long since been obliterated, Valley caught him. He crashed on Valley's seventeen-yards directly in front of the posts.

The madness of the stands became mad frenzy.

"Joe!" Tarly gasped. "Take it easy; take your time. Joe, this is your chance."

As coolly, as unconcerned as though this were a practice session, Joe Macy stepped back into kicking position. He took off his headguard and sailed it toward the sideline. Tarly picked it up. Sweat was in Joe's eyes; he ran the sleeve of a dirtied jersey across his face. He balanced himself and tested the ground. His hands went up and made a clear target for the center.

The pass came back to him—perfect. One quick step back with the right foot and then one forward. The foot swung as it came forward. The ball fell, it met his instep solidly, it was in the air. Mountain had made a clean job of blocking and holding. The ball sailed above a sprawled line, tumbled twice in its flight, and fell on a declining arc above the bar and between the goal posts for a field goal.

Oh, the glory of the tumult then! The wild roar of students and graduates who had seen a beaten team snatch victory from defeat!

The waves of insane sound ran through Tarly like a rich, sweet benediction. A strange sweat ran down his face. He put one hand to his eyes. No; they were tears. A hand was again on his shoulder. A strong hand that trembled.

"Not much time left, Tarly," York said. The coolness was gone from his voice. "Less than two minutes."

Tarly stared at him, uncomprehending.

"Less than two minutes," York said again.

"Oh!" The captain nodded. "You won't need me."

"No. It's scarcely worth while going in. After— after that kick I'd like to let Joe finish." He looked at the captain sideways and there was almost an appeal in his eyes.

But what Tarly said had nothing to do with a stricken hope or with disappointment. "Wasn't it great, York?" Never before had the name fallen familiarly from his lips. "Wasn't it? I wouldn't have missed it for anything. It's great—everything."

The victory tumult was wearing itself out from sheer exhaustion. When York spoke his voice was low.

"It is great, Tarly, when you understand."

"I wouldn't have missed a single minute of it for anything in the world," Tarly said again.

"Even though you were kept from your last big game?" York asked, his voice lower still.

The glow in Tarly's eyes deepened as he watched the tired, happy players walking up the field to form for another kick-off.

"I don't think," he said after a silence, "I've given that a thought since the game started."

The stands, the band, had broken into fresh song.

"Mountain won more than one victory today,"

York said, and now his voice was like the clear, high call of a bugle.

They walked up the field together—the man who had brought a new spirit to Mountain High and the captain who had found that spirit.

THE END